"A beautifully written and ev— — —re and destructive power of love—ror— — —places we call and have called home. Goodison finds a glittering and urgent beauty in the everyday, without shying away from a frank confrontation of those moments when the everyday is shattered by trauma."

—Danielle Evans, author of *Before You Suffocate Your Own Fool Self,* winner of the PEN/Robert W. Bingham Prize

"*By Love Possessed* is a terrific book. I love the tender beautiful writing; I love the characters, and in many ways it felt as if I had met them before. How Lorna Goodison manages to capture so much about human complexities in these stories is baffling. I just love this book."

—Uwem Akpan, author of *Say You're One of Them*, an Oprah Book Club selection

"Few writers are as attuned as Goodison to the heartaches and triumphs of Jamaicans, especially Jamaican women. . . . Fewer writers still tell us so much about what it means to be human. Written by the hand of a poet, the prose in this collection is consistently beautiful."

—Elizabeth Nunez, author of *Prospero's Daughter* and *Boundaries*

"Halfway through Lorna Goodison's stunning collection *By Love Possessed*, I realized I was holding my breath. This was partly because of the uniqueness of the subject matter . . . [and] partly because of the uniqueness of style: a cool, faintly decorous prose, incorporating a witty, intelligent, idiosyncratic Jamaican language. . . . For Goodison, the story is a virtuosic performance; full of glorious lyrics, mystical dreams and mesmerizing seascapes." —*Globe and Mail*

"After reading *By Love Possessed*, an elegant, soulful collection . . . I spent the rest of 2011 tracking down everything [of Goodison's] I could find. Rare is my introduction to an author so rewarding. Goodison is a gem."

—*National Post*

Also by Lorna Goodison

NONFICTION

From Harvey River

POETRY

Selected Poems
To Us, All Flowers Are Roses
Turn Thanks
Travelling Mercies
Controlling the Silver
Goldengrove: New and Selected Poems

LORNA GOODISON

By Love Possessed

Stories

Amistad
An Imprint of HarperCollins*Publishers*

To Ted, with love

Acknowledgement of any prior publication of these stories appears on page 263.

BY LOVE POSSESSED. Copyright © 2011 by Lorna Goodison. All rights reserved. Printed in the United States of America. No part of this book may be used or reproduced in any manner whatsoever without written permission except in the case of brief quotations embodied in critical articles and reviews. For information address HarperCollins Publishers, 10 East 53rd Street, New York, NY 10022.

HarperCollins books may be purchased for educational, business, or sales promotional use. For information please write: Special Markets Department, HarperCollins Publishers, 10 East 53rd Street, New York, NY 10022.

First published in Canada in 2011 by McClelland & Stewart Ltd., Toronto, Ontario.

FIRST U.S. EDITION

Library of Congress Cataloging-in-Publication Data has been applied for.

ISBN 978-0-06-212735-8

12 13 14 15 16 OV/RRD   10 9 8 7 6 5 4 3 2 1

CONTENTS

The Helpweight

～

A GORGEOUS LANDSCAPE by George Rodney is on dis-
play in the foyer outside the main dining room. She
stops and carefully admires it for at least four minutes before
making her way over to where he is sitting by himself at,
she could not believe his nerve, their old table. Their old
table in the corner where the lavender blossoms of a lignum
vitae tree created their own painting framed by the mahog-
any trim of the window.

He is much heavier now and his 1960s afro is gone, taking
with it an inch or two of his hairline. Their friends at Excelsior
High School who used to call him King Quarter Past Midnight
would no doubt notice that English winters have rendered
him at least a shade lighter. Gone is the blue-black sheen, but
his profile still looks like it could have been stamped on a
coin, with those hooded eyes and what their History teacher
once described as his Augustan nose. "Ah, Mr. Nathan Aiken,
he of the Augustan – that is, large – nose, who is staring out
the window even as I speak."

It is now an older Nathan who is sitting there in the Hummingbird Restaurant, staring out the window. His navy-blue suit worn with a blue-white shirt and striped tie is no doubt the suit from Savile Row he always said he would have built by a bespoke tailor when he was called to the bar. But she looked good too, considering.

"Hail Queen, live forever. Live forever, O my Queen. I, your lowly subject, have taken the liberty of ordering your special gin and tonic – mostly tonic with a teaspoon of gin. I'm really proud of myself for remembering that. Your Majesty, your shrimp cocktail starter and curried lobster main course await you. Is your long-lost consort good or what?"

She calmly addresses the waiter:

"A campari and soda please, and I'd like to have a look at the menu."

"But . . ."

For the first time since she sat down at the table she stares him fully in the face. He looks sheepish and embarrassed at her blunt refusal to enter into their old game, and then right there in the presence of the waiter she says:

"Nathan, you are a dog, and having said that, please, please don't bother with the walk down memory lane because you will definitely be walking alone. I'm only here for the free lunch and to stop you from pestering me on the telephone. When you came back to Jamaica, you called and said you were asking me for just one favour, so I gave you the name of my real estate agent and she found you your four-bedroom Hillview townhouse. What more, in the name of Jesus, could you want from me now?"

"Don't start beating me up yet. At least wait till you've ordered."

"So what about the two swims cocktail, sir?"

"Just bring them. I'll eat them."

The waiter, who looks a little like Cyril, the stupid busboy from the play *Smile Orange*, saunters off in the direction of the kitchen. They sit in silence until the Cyril lookalike returns bearing two wide-lipped cocktail glasses each with six limp shrimps hooked over the rims.

"Your swims cocktail, sir." He places them in the centre of the table.

The damp pink shrimps look as if they are clinging for dear life to the rim of the glasses, which are stuffed with icy lettuce.

"I'll have the smoked marlin for my appetizer, and then the steamed red snapper, thank you."

He tells the waiter to cancel the order of curried lobster.

"I know, I made my bed, so I'm the one who has to lie in it. Freudian slip, right? Don't laugh, please, you are the one woman, the one woman in the world, I've ever loved, and trust me, that is never going to change. The human equivalent of the cockroach, that's me, maybe even the drummer roach, but I just can't see the two of us living in Jamaica and not speaking to each other. Remember our song? 'Friends and Lovers Forever'?"

She kisses her teeth.

"I never intended to marry anybody but you! I know you don't want to hear this, but only God knows how."

"If this is what you called me here to tell me, I am leaving right now!"

"No, please, just hear me out, there is not a day that I don't find a reason to mention your name to somebody. A few hours ago I told a lawyer who just got back from Egypt that I was going to have lunch with this fabulous woman who looks like an Egyptian queen."

"Nathan, to tell you the truth, our story? That is history. Call it water under Flat Bridge if you want, so let's cut out the rubbish. What did you really call me here for?"

"I want you to be friends with my wife, Deidra. She has no friends in Jamaica. Please take her shopping for me."

Back at her office she calls her sister and tells her what just happened.

"So what did you tell him?"

"To kiss my royal arse."

"I know you invited me to kiss your arse, and believe me I would gladly kiss any part of your perfect body, but yesterday in the restaurant when I tried to give you a little peck, just the tiniest peck on your cheek, you informed me that I was never ever to touch you again. Hello, hello?

"This is your old school friend Nathan calling to remind you that when we were in first form together I used to bring paradise plums and put them on your desk and you used to fling them back at me and tell me how you didn't want any sweeties from me. But I want to remind you that I just kept putting them on your desk anyway. Please don't hang up . . . hello?"

"Yes, yes, that is true I have no mind, no mind whatsoever and please, please, don't hang up the phone again, for I, Nathan-no-mind-Aitken, am begging you to please take Deidra shopping for me. The bar association banquet is Saturday night and when she showed me what she intends to wear, I decided to subject myself to any form of humiliation and to ask you, no, beg you, to please take her shopping for me, and please take her to a good hairdresser."

She sits in a high-backed wicker chair on the balcony of her new upper St. Andrew townhouse. She is dressed in a close-fitting linen shift that is the colour of black coffee. Apart from her gold stud earrings, she is wearing only one other piece of jewellery, a strand of blue and gold beads. Her hair is newly relaxed and pinned in a smooth knot on top of her head. She has outlined her almond-shaped eyes with a kohl pencil, dusted her high forehead and her perfect nose with shimmering bronze face powder, and applied gloss to her lips that Nathan used to say tasted like naseberries. Her nails are done in a subtle shade of copper and her narrow size-seven-and-a-half feet are bare except for two jewelled toe rings. He will see again what he missed when he arrives with his wife.

Her fragrance was like a divine breath, her scent reached as far as the land of Punt; her skin is made of gold, it shines like the stars in the halls of festival, in the view of the whole land.

Queen Hatshepsut had written that about herself. It was said to be the only example in Egyptian history of a woman describing herself. When Nathan first went to England, he had sent her a postcard with an image of Hatshepsut and that quotation on it. The postcard was still somewhere in her storeroom in a box of photographs and letters.

"You are a damn idiot, you must be the only person in the world who hasn't heard that black is beautiful." That is what she had told a girl at Excelsior High School who had had the nerve to ask her why she was going around with a boy as black as Nathan.

The girl had said, "My god, all him hand-middle black! How you children going to look?"

Soon after that she started to wear her hair in an afro, and she and Nathan had formed a Black Studies group with other "conscious" students. They met on Friday evenings after school and taught themselves about ancient black civilizations. The both of them had also taken to going by bus out to Cable Hut Beach. They would lie on a big towel in the sand and rub baby oil over each other and when things became too hot, they would hot step across the sand and dash into the sea to cool off. On Mondays they'd return to school and show off their "tans" to the other sixth formers. "If Nathan is King Quarter Past Midnight then I'm Queen Quarter to Twelve."

Deidra gets out of the car and immediately bends down and hugs and kisses the dog that belongs to the retired couple who live in the adjoining townhouse. As she told her sister afterwards, you could easily imagine Deidra sitting on a three-legged stool milking a cow. Deidra who turns out to be a stout country girl with freckles and a full head of reddish-brown curls. Deidra who is dressed in what seems to be the preferred look of some Englishwomen who come to live in the Caribbean, a pastel floral print dress and open-toed white sandals. She firmly extends a hand to Nathan's wife, Deidra, at the door; there will be no kissing, especially after she just hugged up that dog. She fixes him with a venomous look when he leans in to kiss her cheek and says, "I really appreciate your doing this."

The helper comes in and passes round crystal glasses of watermelon juice once the three of them are seated in the living room.

"Man, these paintings are brilliant," says Nathan. "Are they all by the same artist?"

"Yes, they're by Patrick Waldemar."

"Nefertiti or Hatshepsut?" Nathan has seated himself next to a mahogany pedestal and is gently stroking the face of the terracotta head displayed on it.

"Nefertiti?"

"It's by Gene Pearson."

He slides lower into the antique mahogany loveseat.

"You're going to have to show us how to get an art collection together. I hear that it's you who convinced Royal Bank to invest in Jamaican art. Deidra, this lady here is one very successful marketing manager."

Deidra smiles and looks around the room and murmurs softly, "Lovely, so lovely."

She looks at her watch.

"I guess you ladies want to get going, eh?"

"Yes, I have to be back here before twelve."

He stands up and hands her, not Deidra, a signed blank cheque, he looks at her, not Deidra, and says, "Thank you,

you hear, thank you. Could you just call me when you are finished and I'll come and pick her up." Nathan's wife smiles nervously when they get into her company car, which is brand new and smells discreetly of sandalwood, and she apologizes for tracking dirt onto the beige carpet with her white sandals.

"So what part of England are you from?"

"Good heavens noo, I'm from Ireland, but I met up with Nate when he was a student chap and I was working over in London. Sure me dad would spit bullets if he heard that anyone mistook mi for an Englishwoman."

Polite question number two, and how did she like Jamaica?

"Ah, lovely but sooo hot, and the mosquitoes are far for sure too friendly, and I hope you'll not think me rude or anything, but this whole shopping excursion is Nate's idea, and I'd just as soon wear something I brought with me, but maybe we could not stop out too long? You see I've decided that we'll not be employing a maid. Jayzus, I'm home all day, what would I be needing a maid for, and my mother always said, 'If you keep your house, your house will keep you.'" Once Deidra starts talking she can't seem to stop.

"And I want to bake some soda bread for his tea, quite fond of my soda bread he's become, and I want to make sure his shirt's pressed proper for tonight. His mam showed me how he liked his shirts pressed, she lives with us now you know, she's got the diabetes, the poor thing, and that's another reason why I can't stop out too long."

Deidra looks out on a small boy who offers to wipe the windshield when they come to the traffic lights at Manor Park:

"Jayzus, poor mite."

Yes, that is what Deidra says now, but she will soon be sunning herself by the pool with the other ex-pat women and bitching about "the damn lazy maid" who was inside slaving over her and Nathan's four-bedroom interior designer–decorated Hillview townhouse.

"I'm also volunteering at Sister O'Riley's children's home downtown. Jayzus, the poor little mites."

The week before he'd gone off to law school in England, she and Nathan were at their table by the window at the Hummingbird.

"Look, I know you've definitely made up your mind to stay here and go to University at Mona, but please, just think again about coming to join me in England after I've settled? You could come and we could have a small wedding and —"

"We're not going over this again! What would I do in England while you're studying? Work as a bus conductress on London transport?"

"Don't look at it like that. We'd be working, as my mother would say, 'to make life.' Look, I know myself, I not good at the cooking and washing and ironing business. But it's not just that, England is cold, you know!"

He had reached under the table and stroked her thigh when he said that. She had yanked down the hem of her miniskirt.

After he was gone, she had visited his mother every week for almost a year.

"Mi say, you have to take a cushion and stuff inna the sleeve so iron it, because if Nathan see one crease inna him sleeve, him wet it up and iron it out himself.

"I telling you these things so that when you and him married, you know how fi care him." And then he had stopped writing, and then one day she had gone to take his mother to do her banking and to pay her electricity bill and his mother had cried and told her that Nathan had finally written to say that six months ago he had married a white girl but he didn't know how to tell her.

When her sister heard about Nathan's marriage, she'd said:

"These women are usually the landladies' daughters, you know. It's like they've died and gone to heaven when they get one of these Jamaican men who go away to study law or medicine to marry them and bring them back to Jamaica. And as soon as they reach here and start living big life, these women, who used to be maids where they come from, start to go on as if they better than you and me!"

She is fine now. She is completely over Nathan. She is dating a doctor who has been talking about getting serious. She is fine. She no longer has to fight the impulse to drive out to Cable Hut Beach, park her car, get out and walk past the spot where she and Nathan used to lie together, and just keep walking straight out into deep sea. She does not want to dig up any old story of how the man whose beautiful, gifted, and black children she thought she would have had by now had married an Irish chambermaid who had washed his clothes and cooked his food and warmed his bed when he was a struggling law student.

When they arrived at the My Fair Lady Boutique and Beauty Salon, Deidra headed straight for a floral caftan. She was tempted to tell her "Yes, my dear, go ahead and buy it, it suits you," but Nathan knew her well; she was not the kind of woman who would ever deliberately lead somebody astray.

"You know what will really suit you, this black dress."

"Ah rich black." Deidra lightly touches the hem of the blue-black crepe sheathe.

"Remind me again, why do they call Ireland the Emerald Isle?"

And Deidra's big greenish-brown eyes are full of water as she lowers her voice and says, "Because where I'm from, the land is so green, a green as can break your heart like a lover, so beautiful it is."

"Well, since you are from the Emerald Isle, you should get these green satin pumps and handbag to go with this black dress, and I suggest that you get two of these Irish linen dresses because I'm sure you'll be going with your husband to business lunches."

Deidra buys the handbag but declines the green satin pumps, saying the heels are too high for her.

The flowers came while she was away in Negril with the doctor who now wants to get really serious. The helper put the extravagant arrangement of orchids and roses on the dresser in her bedroom, a good thing too, for when they got back into Kingston on Sunday evening, the doctor only managed to come as far as the living room when his beeper went off and he had to leave because one of his patients had gone into labour. The minute she saw the flowers, she knew. "You know what," her sister said, "you should let me call his house and ask for Deidra. I'll tell her I'm your sister and that you asked me to tell her thanks for the flowers." The doctor has never sent her flowers. The doctor always smells faintly of antiseptic.

"There is a Mr. Nathan Aiken at the gate to see you, ma'am, the same gentleman who was here with a white lady some weeks a back. I must let him through?"

"What the hell you think you're doing coming here uninvited at this time of night?"

He just stands there in her doorway with tears running down his face.

She is not sure what to do. He has come in and seated himself in the mahogany loveseat.

She positions herself in the doorway between the living room and the kitchen and stands there tying and retying the sash of her dressing gown. Finally she turns and goes into the kitchen. She reaches up into the top cupboard for one of her crystal glasses, decides against it, and picks out one of the plastic ones stamped with Disney characters that she keeps for the times her little niece comes to visit. She hesitates before the refrigerator, traces the Amana logo with her forefinger three times before she opens it, and pours a glass of water from one of the water jugs.

"Here, drink this."

Instead of taking the glass he grabs her around her hips, pulls her to him, and presses his head against her belly.

"My mother!"

When she'd told her sister that she'd agreed to help Nathan organize his mother's funeral, her sister had gone off. "You are mad, stark raving mad! After all that that boy put you through you are still making him use you? So what the hell happen to Deidri or Deidro or whatever the hell the wife name?"

"I'm only helping him with the arrangements for church. It's going to be at St. Mary's in Rollington Town and I've ordered one hundred white chrysanthemums to decorate the altar."

"Chrysanthemums! I bet Nathan's mother never even know what name so!"

"No, that is not true. I used to take her to flower shows."

"My sister, it's like you don't have any mind."

"Look, just leave me, I'm only doing this for his mother. She was always very nice to me."

"Not as nice as you're being to her and her son."

In the church that she decorated with one hundred chrysanthemums, she watches as Deidra, wearing her rich-black dress, sits with one stout arm firmly around her husband's shoulders. Her equally stout husband, Nathan, who manages to compose himself enough to wipe his face with a snowy-white handkerchief and deliver an eloquent remembrance of his mother, now bears little resemblance to her high-school sweetheart, King Quarter Past Midnight. She is not sure how to describe the man standing before the coffin who speaks with a modified English accent about his beloved mother who had sacrificed endlessly. The man who declares that he and his wife, Deidra, would forever mourn the loss of his mother's presence in their home. The man who without a glance in her direction ends by thanking "all the kind friends" who helped and supported him and his dear wife in their time of grief. When he says that, her sister, who had accompanied her to the funeral, leans over, hugs her, and says:

"Kind friend, I think we should leave now and avoid the trip to the cemetery."

Two days after the funeral he shows up at her office. She tells her assistant that she is too busy to see him.

"Tell her I'll wait."

"He says he'll wait."

"He's been sitting outside for an hour and a half now."

"Sorry, he doesn't have an appointment and I have to finish this report."

"He's been out there all afternoon. The personnel officer just called me to ask why we've allowed a member of the public to be sitting out there so long."

"Oh God. Show him in."

"I missed you at the graveside and at the reception."

"I left right after they closed the coffin. I figure I had done my part as one of your kind friends."

"I know, I know. I can't thank you enough for everything, but that is not why I've been sitting outside your office for over three hours. You don't want to hear, but I have to explain to you today why I married Deidra."

Long story. Long story about how he got a terrible flu that turned into bronchitis and because he had nobody to look after him, it was Deidra who was working at the place where he was renting a room, who found him when he had fallen face down in his own vomit on the landing late one night on his way back from the toilet. Deidra who was so strong that she was able to lift him back up two flights of stairs to his room and get him into bed.

"If it wasn't for her I would have died right there, for the landlady was a deaf, colour-prejudiced old bitch who was always banging on, I swear to you, about how the sun, oh the sun had truly set on the British Empire. No doubt because she felt she was reduced to having a man as black as me living in her old house."

"Nathan, how does any of this affect me?"

"No, please, just let me finish. Deidra's father and her brothers are hardcore IRA. They threatened to kill Deidra if she ever came back home and one of them actually paid me a visit. I won't go into what happened, but we got married. She is dead to them. She doesn't have anybody but me, and she cannot go back to Ireland. She . . . Deidra took, takes, very good care of me."

"Well good for you!"

"But it's you I love. Nobody but you. You know me, I'm never going to stop begging you to love me again."

She closes her eyes and sees gun-toting IRA men. The gun-toting IRA men are then replaced by a statue of stout, freckle-faced Deidra half-carrying Nathan up the stairs. *Helpweight.* She suddenly remembers the word she has been looking for to describe this Nathan. Her helper once used it to describe the deadbeat father of her children.

"Him is not a helpmate, ma'am, him is a helpweight. All him do is help weigh me down." Nathan has become her helpweight.

"So, let me get this story straight: you only married Deidra because you were afraid her ignorant gunman relatives would kill you; and she cannot go back to where she came from because she is afraid they will kill her for taking up with a black man, and so you want me to help you to bear your crosses by becoming what? Your Jamaican concubine?"

"Don't put it like that. It will never be like that. You are number one, you will always be the queen."

"Nathan, go on home to your wife. I'm sure she has some soda bread or soda dumpling that she cooked today ready and waiting for you after she ironed your shirt without any seam in the sleeves. You just look at me good —"

"I can't take my eyes off you. That blouse, it's raw silk, right? You, my love, should wear royal purple every day of life."

"Nathan, all that is so old. Old, tired, and pathetic. I could never, never stoop so low as to eat Deidra's what-left. And since you won't leave, I'm leaving, and you can stay here and explain to Royal Bank just what you are doing in my office."

She will tell the doctor that she too now wants to get very serious.

She will drive home to her beautifully appointed townhouse past the guard at the gate to whom she will issue instructions that he is never to let Mr. Nathan Aitken through to her again. She will take her telephone off the hook. Tomorrow she will call the telephone company and arrange to get an unlisted number. She will get the box of his cards and letters and photographs from the storeroom and she will run them through the shredder in her home office. She will never wear that purple silk blouse ever again. She will give away the terracotta bust he touched that first time he came into her living room. She will sell the mahogany chair he sat in. She will never again set foot inside the Hummingbird Restaurant. She will systematically erase every image, every trace of Nathan Aitken – who had the unmitigated gall to suggest that she settle for being his concubine – from her life. That is what they did to heretic kings in ancient Egypt.

Jamaica Hope

COW BREDDA is what people called T.P. Lecky because he was so good at breeding cattle. The brother of cows had done some science and cross-bred different cattle to come up with the big champion animals called the Jamaica Hope that were taller than most men and bigger than the governor's washing tub.

The first time Lilla saw Alphanso, he had been viewing the Jamaica Hope cattle at the Denbigh Agricultural Show. Tall, cocoa-coloured, and slim, he had worn dungarees and a white shirt and a straw hat like a busha. He stood there perfectly still, gazing at the massive red bulls, his arms folded across his chest and his head tilted to one side. She had gone over to stand beside him and said:

"What a big bull cow!"

"So bull and man must stay. Wait, wait, smile again and make me see. Oh, so you're a bag a sugar gal!"

"Me? What you mean, 'bag a sugar'?"

"You never hear the calypso by the Mighty Sparrow? A girl like you with space between her front teeth is a bag a sugar gal."

She'd liked how he looked right into her eyes when he said that; and because he had given her a reason to smile, she just kept smiling when he invited her to walk around the show grounds and see the sights of Denbigh with him. The next week she went and joined the May Pen 4H Club because he had told her that he was a member. In the home economics classes she learned how to cook, bake, and sew and to make jellies and preserves; eventually she became the best pickle-maker in the entire parish of Clarendon.

Lilla uses a penknife to artfully carve little fishes from chocho, pumpkins, sweet peppers, and carrots, then slice thin strips of cucumber skins to create water weeds. The small whole onions she drops into the brine look like smooth shells in a vinegar and salt sea, and the bright red and yellow Scotch bonnet peppers look like tropical coral. The judges always award her first prize at the annual agricultural show.

This is one of the things she does to make money; she makes pickles and sells them to the supermarket, and she does crochet, embroidery, and straw work, all of which she learned when she joined the 4H Club, where she had pledged her head, hands, heart, and hopes not so much to the building of her community but to building a life with Alphanso.

~

When the first week of July comes around, he packs his carpenter's toolbox and walks the five miles up to the Denbigh showground. He leaves at about seven in the morning. When Lilla does not see him return by eleven, she fixes his lunch in a three-tiered enamel carrier and walks up to the showground. Except for the big red-blossomed poinciana trees – it was as if they drank heat the way other plants drank water, swallowing the heat and then spitting out fire flowers – the other trees and flowers along the way look beaten down, humbled by the sun. She is glad that she remembered to walk with her straw hat that has the plaid ribbon around the crown. She had made the hat herself, to sell to a woman who sold straw goods in Ocho Rios market, but she'd liked it so much that she'd kept it. The hat suits her heart-shaped face with her full brown eyes and her short straight nose. When she arrives at Denbigh, she finds him standing by a big four-wheel drive vehicle that has Ace Fertilizer lettered on the side panels. A tense-looking young woman is seated in the driver's seat; Lilla overhears her telling Alphanso through the open window of the van:

"Look, I'm a woman who doesn't joke. When I say I want my business done in a certain way, I really mean it. I want this to be the best booth at Denbigh this year."

Lilla can see from Alphanso's face that he was not really listening. She could have told the young woman that all she had to do was to provide the materials and leave the plan for the display booth and he would get the job done. He had been working at Denbigh for years. In the last week of July he would often work around the clock on six or seven different booths at the same time, and he always charged more for last-minute work.

When he looks up and sees Lilla, he nods and gives her a half-smile, and she smiles her wide smile. He knows that she has brought his lunch of hard food. Alphanso has to have hard food every day. Thick slices of boiled yam and green bananas; broad, elastic flour dumplings and some kind of fish or meat, washed down with her special lemonade made from wet sugar and Seville oranges.

"Drink it before the ice melt out," she tells him. She had stopped at the gate and bought a piece of ice from the sno-cone man and dropped it into the jar. He takes up his toolbox and tells the overbearing Kingston woman, "I will meet you right here next week Wednesday at ten o'clock when you bring the materials. I'm going to eat my lunch now."

The tinted window of the van shoots up when Alphanso says that and the tense woman disappears from view. Alphanso quickly steps back as the engine starts up and the van speeds off, kicking up clouds of grey dust.

Lilla and Alphanso go and sit under one of the big lignum vitae trees on the Denbigh showground. He sits down on his wooden toolbox, and she stands behind him and watches how his shoulders hunch forward as he bites into the thick flour dumplings.

She sees for the first time that the hair on top of his head is thinning. Of late, when he works long and hard, she has to boil soursop-leaf tea for him to make him sleep. Ten years they have been together, they have two children living and one little girl who died from a hole in the heart. Everybody says that she was one of the prettiest babies they had ever seen. Although Lilla had cried night and day for weeks after the baby's death, Alphanso never cried. Even when he had to make the coffin for his own child, and lift it up, and put her and the coffin in the grave that he same one helped to dig under the June plum tree in the yard, he never cried.

Alphanso, I think we should get married. Or, Alphanso, you don't think is time me and you get married now? Or . . . Alphanso, you don't think that after everything that me and you go through we must get married?

She is still there trying to decide what is the best way to say what she wants to say when he finishes eating and gets up off the toolbox and says:

"Thank you for the lunch, Lilla. See you later on."

He walks off toward another group of Kingston people who have arrived and are standing in shock next to a permanent booth that had been occupied by a madman for the past few months. It would need to be built over almost from scratch as the walls were now black and furry with soot from his cooking fires. Alphanso would make good money from that.

He did not come home until after nine that night.

"What happen, Lilla? You gone to sleep already? Mind you getting old before you time you know, a young man like me can't have no old woman!"

"Which part of you young, Alphanso?"

"Make me show you, no?"

Afterwards as they lie there wrapped together in the double bed that he had built for them from blue mahoe wood, she thinks that now would be a good time to say it out loud. "You don't think is time we get married now?"

He responded with a loud snore.

As she watched the peenie wallies that have flown in through the open window letting their little lights shine in the darkness of their bedroom, she is thinking how every year when he worked at Denbigh, they had used the money to do something special. Over the years they had added to the house with the money that he earned from building and repairing display booths for the annual agricultural show that took place during the first week in August. The rest of the year he did regular carpentry work.

Over the years they have added on to the house with the Denbigh money. It now has three rooms, and they have upgraded the kitchen from a lean-to in the backyard to where it is now firmly attached to the house. They built on a front veranda and bought a two-burner gas stove with it. Three years ago they used the money to pay for the doctor bills for the little girl. This year Alphanso wanted to buy a Jamaica Hope calf. She wanted him to use the Denbigh money to pay for their wedding.

She thinks about how Alphanso and herself would not sleep together the night before their morning wedding in cool December. He would stay with his friend Tipper that night, for it was bad luck for the groom to see the bride in her wedding dress before he saw her in church. Lilla would wake up early and cut a lime in two and use it to wash her skin and cut and clear off all the bad luck of her old life. The dead baby, and all the other mix-up and crosses. After the lime exfoliation, she would bathe with a rose-scented sweet soap. She would dry her plump body with a new towel, put on deodorant, and pat her skin with clouds of dusting powder. The first thing she would put on would be a new blue panty the colour of the morning sky. A blue like a newborn baby's chemise, a blue like the mother of morning had seen her trials and had clipped off a corner of the sky and stitched it into a girdle to help hold her stretched belly-skin firm, to gird her loins in the colour of start-over. She would put on a new brassiere, twin cups of elastic and lace to lift up her breasts, which had dropped three inches after three babies, then her sheer stockings in a shade called cinnamon spice, a white full slip with broad bands of lace scalloping around the hem, lace on top of lace, for brides could never wear too much lace. Then she would sit at the vanity crafted by Alphanso from blue mahoe wood while her sister who was a hairdresser fixed her hair and her makeup.

Not too much, for Alphanso hated makeup. "War-paint," he called it. But after all, this was her wedding day, she would have to powder her face and put on some lipstick, then blot most of it off, so that her lips would look ripe and rosy like the young girl Alphanso had fallen in love with. The bag a sugar gal, who would finally step into her brand-new shoes before she slipped on her satin and lace wedding dress. Everything she had on would be new except for her grandmother's old lace handkerchief that she would tuck into her bosom. Her brother would come to the house and take pictures of her while she dressed. Pictures of her, the bag a sugar gal putting on powder and lipstick at her vanity.

The week before the wedding, she would clean out the house and throw away anything that was too old and shabby, and then she would burn some rosemary leaves on top of the stove so that its righteous smell would waft through their little house and drive away any lingering bad spirits. On the day before, she would shift the bed to a different spot in the room and put the mattress out to sun before she made it up with crisp new sheets.

No, she didn't want to have a big wedding like her aunt who got married when she was nearly sixty years old, in a big white bridal gown with a long floating veil over her hard face, although she had seven children and fifteen grandchildren. But Lilla does want this to truly be her special day. She had decided that she would not make the dress herself although she could sew, but she would give it out to Maud, of Maud's Establishment of Dressmaking in the May Pen Plaza. Not a soul knew this, but she had cut out a style that she liked from *Brides* magazine and folded it into her Bible at the chapter in St. Matthew where Jesus went to the wedding at Cana and turned water into wine.

She was undecided as to whether to wear a short veil, a "fingertip veil," it said in the bridal book, or a mantilla, although she was not really a Catholic, but no matter what, she wanted to carry a bouquet, a nice bunch of roses. Alphanso would have to get his tailor to build him a new suit, and the children would get new clothes and shoes, and the wedding reception would be held at Lilla's mother's seven-bedroom house with enough curry goat and chicken for everyone to eat a belly full.

Because she was almost as good at cake-making as she was at pickle-making, Lilla would bake and decorate the cake herself. If it was going to be a really rich fruit cake, she should buy the raisins and currants and prunes and cherries and start soaking them in red wine and white rum from now because she intended to be Mrs. Alphanso Wills before Christmas.

The mix-up and crosses with Shirnetta had happened some months after the baby died. She had asked him about it when people started telling her things. In any case she had begun to notice how he was pulling away from her in little ways. Any good woman can tell when her man is straying.

Some nights he would come home and go directly to the shower and spend a good twenty minutes washing himself with Lifebuoy soap before he came to bed. Then he would pretend to fall asleep right away and because he was giving Shirnetta money, sometimes he would say he was broke when Lilla asked him for something. But he always denied it when she asked him about him and Shirnetta. Her sister told her:

"As long as him hiding him wrongs from you that mean him still respect you. Is if him look in you face and tell you 'Yes, so what?' that you know that things gone beyond repair."

"So how I hear that you and Shirnetta was buying grocery Friday?"

"I don't know who could a tell you that. You like listen to news carrier too much. Anyway, see I bring something for you here."

"Why? Because you conscience riding you?"

Sometimes she had thought about going to fight Shirnetta, but Alphanso hated scandal. She knew that he would be bound to leave her if she went and did something like that. She decided to leave him after that day in the market when her mother pointed out to her just how she bad she was looking because she was worrying over Alphanso.

"Lilla? But my god in heaven, lookya! Lilla, a really you this?"

"Yes, Mama. I just going to the butcher stall to buy some mutton for Alphanso dinner."

"And you come out of you house, walk come clear a market inna that tear-down hem, wash-out, mash-up-like-a-callaloo old frock? With your hair like a bird nest underneath Alphanso old hat? And why the hell you wearing Alphanso old bruk-down counter shoes? When I see you passing my stall I had was to look twice. Me say to myself, God see and know that could never be my daughter, not that half-mad careless woman!"

"Alphanso, me a leave you."

"Leave who?"

"You. Go on go live with leather-back Shirnetta. You not mashing me down any further. I am taking my two children and I am going back to my mother house."

Two weeks later he had come around to her mother's house and asked to see her.

"Lilla, I want you to come home."

"What happen? Rum-glass Shirnetta keeping man with you?"

"Rest the Shirnetta business, man. This is me and you business."

"Why I must come back and make you and you frowsy-tail Jezebel have me as Clarendon laughing stock?"

When she said that, he hung down his head and said in a low voice:

"I done with her. Is you is my rightful woman. Just come home."

"I will see how I feel, but make I tell you this. From now, if I ever hear that you even tell Miss iron-front how-de-do again, as God liveth, I never talk to you again in life."

A few weeks later, she had taken the children and gone back to him, to the disgust of her mother, who always said of herself:

"Me a one big independent woman. Me no haffi put up with foolishness from man, as them bother me two time, I run them backside."

After she came back to Alphanso, Lilla heard that Shirnetta had gone to New York. Now the news around May Pen is that she was coming back to Jamaica in December.

"Alphanso, wake up, wake up, man. I have something to say to you."

"What, what? Is thief?"

"No, is me. I want to get married."

"What is this? You wake me up out of my deep, deep sleep fi tell me bout get married?"

"Yes, is time now!"

He didn't say anything when she said that, but at least she knew that he had heard.

"Bob, hear my crosses now, Lilla want get married."

"All woman want to get married."

"You know how much people live good good then them go and get married and everything crash?"

"Mama, Alphanso don't want get married."
   "No man in Jamaica ever want get married."

From before she proposed to Alphanso, Lilla had started to fix up herself. Everybody was telling her how she was looking nice. She had sewn some new dresses for herself, had thrown away Alphanso's mash-down counter shoes and ordered a pair of sandals from the Rasta man. She painted her toenails hibiscus pink and made herself two pairs of Bermuda shorts.

"Alphanso, I'm going take out a passport."
   "Take out passport fi what? Fi go where?"
   "I going try my luck – see if I get a visa to Canada, although everybody say the Canadian Embassy harder than the American one."
   "And what about me and the two children?"
   "My mother will look after them. You're a big man, you can manage."
   Alphanso kissed his teeth.

In the second week of July when things start to get really busy at Denbigh, Lilla tells Alphanso:
   "I can't bring no lunch today, I have some business to take care of in town. You better get something light."
   Something light? Something light? From the day of his birth Alphanso had never eaten light food. His mother brought

up her sons on hard food. He had to have hard food to balance him while he was doing all that heavy carpentry work. Light food? He knows what Lilla is trying to do, she is trying to force his hand. But he is a man, he can't let her do this to him.

"You can't make a dame run your life. It's you supposed to ask her to marry, not the other way around."

That is what Cowboy Bob, Alphanso's brother, tells him. Bob is called Cowboy Bob because he went away to do farm-work and stayed in America for years. When he came back, all he had to show for years of hard work was a high cowboy hat, a pair of knee-deep water boots, and a transistor radio.

"I'm telling you, Phanso boy, that Yankee woman that I married was sweet as cherry pie, nice like a pound of rice until I put that ring on her finger, then bam! She start to treat me like a dog. As a matter of fact, she treat the dog better than me. Many is the day I see her kiss that mongrel bitch when she wouldn't make me touch her. She never stop till she drive me out of my own house that I work like a mule to buy. She take me to the cleaners, man, take me to the cleaners."

"You woulda never see me, Alphanso Wills, in a situation like that, for is me run tings, tings don't run me. Anyhow, who tell you say a countryman like you from Clarendon, Jamaica, could a manage a big, experience, Yankee woman?"

From the day that the Yankee woman divorced him, Bob lived cowboy life. He never lived with a woman ever again. He had come back to Jamaica and built a little house above where Lilla and Alphanso lived. They would hear him going home at night to his little "ranch" as he called his one-roomed wooden house, accompanied only by the night breeze carrying the wailing refrains of the country-and-western songs he crooned in his rum-soaked Jamerican accent.

When things start to get busy at Denbigh, the loudmouth woman with the Ace Fertilizer booth just won't give Alphanso a break to hustle and do his five other booths. Two days now he is reduced to eating patty and coco bread and bun and cheese because Lilla has gone into Kingston to the passport office. Lilla who comes home from the passport office late and in a taxi that drops her off at the gate. She stays outside for what seems like a long time talking to the taximan. When Alphanso asks her what she was out there doing so long, she says that the taximan did not have enough change. Alphanso tells her:

"Well maybe you should just go on back to Kingston with your taximan."

Later in bed he says, "Lilla, is not that I don't want to be married to you, is just that I . . . Lilla, don't believe I don't love you . . . You know is just that sometime I can't understand what happening to me . . . I was always a strong man . . . but these days me no understand why me feel so . . . The girl from town handle me like a boy over the booth and I have fi just take it because mi want the money . . . And now you come with this married business. Lilla, is you is mi woman . . . why we don't just go on cool same way?"

Alphanso had not wanted the new baby. He had believed that Lilla was taking birth control. He had not felt as excited over the pregnancy as he had when Lilla was big with the other

LORNA GOODISON

two children, but when he'd seen her at the hospital he couldn't believe how pretty the little girl was. She had looked like she was made out of chocolate and she had had a thick head of hair for a baby and her little eyes were shine as ackee seeds. He had fallen in love. He'd marvelled that Lilla and himself produced a child so perfect. Her lips were the wine colour of an otaheite apple and she looked as if she were wearing lipstick. Later when her life started to seep out of her through the hole in her heart, her lips would turn dark blue, as if she were drinking ink.

For days after the funeral he'd felt as if he was still carrying the baby in his arms. He had actually felt her little head tucked under his chin and the light weight of her body still resting on his chest. That is how she'd liked to fall asleep. She'd made little wheezing, whistling sounds like a fee-fee when she slept, and sometimes she'd laugh out in her sleep, a gurgling little baby laugh. One year after she came into the world, he had had to build a small cedar board box the size of a bureau drawer in which to place her body and to bury her under the June plum tree. Alphanso did not want anything to change in his life again. He wanted everything to continue just as it was.

Lilla starts to sing some serious bantering songs now. Her favourites are the Joe Tex song "Hold On to What You Got" and a medley she has strung together from Cowboy Bob's country-and-western repertoire, in which the lines "I'm moving on" and "You never miss your water till your well runs dry" feature very heavily. Alphanso goes through the gate to the sound of Lilla sitting over the washtub scrubbing and singing. When she sings the part about "*one two three,*" she wrings Alphanso's shirts so hard that it's a wonder they don't all tear into one two three.

"I am married but I don't church." That is what she always says when people ask her about Alphanso and herself. One of the main reasons that Lilla wants to get married is because of something that she heard that Shirnetta said. Somebody had asked Shirnetta what she was doing with Alphanso. If she didn't know that Lilla and Alphanso were practically married and Shirnetta said that Lilla had no talk because she had no ring.

Lilla wants her ring. She wants to feel her left hand grow heavy with gold. She wants her ring finger to get "proud," and to stick out from the other fingers on her hand. She wants to use her be-ringed left hand to languidly wipe her eyes, to wave at her friends, to cover her mouth when she yawns. She wants to get to sit in the front seat beside the driver and tap out a triumphant, ringing golden rhythm with her wedding band on the solid frame of a moving vehicle.

During the last week of July, things get really busy up at Denbigh for the show that takes place during the first week of August, Independence weekend. The Monday morning, Alphanso's business is nearly completely spoiled because he goes to finish the booths and Bob does not turn up to help him. Nobody has seen him since last night when he was drinking in Tipper's bar and punching his Marty Robbins songs into the jukebox.

Alphanso has to leave his work at midday to go and see what happened to his brother. When he beats on the door of Bob's ranch, he gets no answer and the windows are closed tight. He finally breaks down the door and sees Bob lying on the ground with his features twisted as if he slept too long with his face turned toward the pulling force of the full moon.

He runs home and gets Lilla, who comes back with him to Bob's house. She immediately takes charge of the situation. They take Bob in a taxi to the May Pen hospital, where the doctors say that he has had a stroke. Lilla goes back home and packs a small suitcase with two pairs of Alphanso's pyjamas, a towel, wash rag, soap, and toothpaste. Bob does not own a pair of pyjamas and the one towel he has, hanging on a nail behind his door, is sour-smelling and stiff as if it is protesting against being used and reused without being washed.

Over the next few days Lilla takes food and clean pyjamas for Bob in the mornings. Alphanso visits him and brings home the used pyjamas each night so that Lilla can wash and iron them. Alphanso tries to thank her and she brushes him off, saying:

"I would do the same for my enemy."

On Thursday the Denbigh show opens and the booth that Alphanso built for the Ace Fertilizer woman wins a prize, but this doesn't really sweet him. He has had to work ten times as hard with Bob not there. He engaged a "prentice" to work with him, but he had to constantly explain to the boy what needed to be done. With Bob, the two of them worked with one mind. If he thought about strengthening a beam, he would look up to see Bob sawing a brace for the beam. Now Bob looks like he will never function fully again. His tongue stirs his words slowly so that he sounds as if he is talking with a mouth full of porridge, but his nose and mouth have come back round more to the centre of his face.

"One hot stout, Tipper."

"Sorry bout Bob, man. Hmm."

"How bout a game a domino?"

"I will take a rain check."

"How Lilla?"

"Putting on the pressure."

"How you feel?"

"Bwoy, Tipper, I don't even know."

"Alphanso, make me tell you why most man married. Man married because them tired. Tired from years of running down woman, tired to get up and leave woman house early morning make dew water wet them. Tired because mortal man cannot take the kind of pressure woman keep up when them decide is time to put on that ring. I don't believe you have one Jamaican man ever willingly get married. Jamaican man married *because them tired.*"

Alphanso leaves the bar and buys a bucket of fried chicken, then he catches a ride in a Lada taxi. Along the way he passes houses like his, protected by green barbed wire fences of dildo macca. When he gets home he sees Lilla outside by the wash line and he goes over to her and hands her the bucket of chicken. Then he does something else, he gives her an envelope thick with five hundred-dollar bills.

"See the money for your wedding here."
"Then is not your wedding too?"
"Anything you want I want."
"You fraid you end up like Bob?"
"Lilla!"
And Lilla smiles her winning bag a sugar gal smile.

Henry

~

MAYBE THE NEXT TIME that the big silver cloud Rolls-Royce comes rolling majestically down the long driveway that is shaded by poinciana and lignum vitae trees, with the police outriders in front sounding the hysterical sirens, it will stop at the intersection of Hope Road and Lady Musgrave Road. The silver cloud will stand still, the rear window will be eased down, and the wife of the Governor General will call out to Henry, singling him out from the twenty or so young men who sell flowers at the gate: "Hello you, you little one in those red corduroy trousers that must be so hot on you, come dear, and let me find a place for you to live. You really should not be out on the street like this."

And Henry is so grateful that he runs to the car and just gives her all his roses. Three dozen pink and four dozen red sweetheart roses. The Governor General's wife smiles gently and reaches through the window to accept this mixed-roses bouquet, then she opens the car door and tells Henry to get in beside her. He climbs in, kisses her on the cheek, and the silver cloud moves off like a winged chariot.

When Henry was a little boy, his mother used to smell like fresh bread to him. His grandmother smelled like garlic, nutmeg, and coconut oil because she was a cook in a restaurant. His grandfather always smelled like cigarettes because he worked at the Machado Tobacco factory, but nothing in his life ever smelled as good to him as the roses. Some nights when he lies down on a piece of foam rubber on the concrete floor in the abandoned house almost opposite the Prime Minister's Office, he tries to remember if anything he knew smelled better than roses. Not aftershave lotion, no matter how good it smelled when you put it on. After a while when you walked up and down hustling in the hot sun, especially if you didn't bathe that day – especially if, like Henry, you had wet your bed the night before – aftershave lotion would turn frowsy on you and begin to follow you around like a bully trying to pick a fight till you began to wish you had just stayed with your own natural body smell.

Sometimes when Henry leaned over to sell roses to some pretty woman in a big air-conditioned car, the scent of their expensive colognes would drift up to him, like a cool Christmas breeze. But these women always looked at him as if he were something that had been spawned at the bottom of their garbage pan, and they would hold their fingers up high and drop the money for the flowers into his palm.

Maybe the only smell that was as good as roses was that of the nutmeg and vanilla in the cornmeal porridge that his grandparents used to cook for him.

Henry is sitting beside the Governor General's wife in the silver car in which the Queen rides when she comes to Jamaica. The scent of the roses that he has presented to the Governor General's wife is so strong that he opens his eyes wide and there he sees all his roses in a plastic bucket by his head. The seven dozen roses, three dozen pink and four dozen red, each dozen girdled round by a transparent shining band of cellophane. The roses look strange in the ramshackle room with no furniture; just some pieces of foam rubber and cardboard flung down on the ground.

Now Henry remembers what happened yesterday. A heavy sheet of rain had fallen and nobody stopped to buy roses. People just rolled their car windows right up and drove hard to get home. Rainy season is bad for the flower-selling business; Christmastime is wonderful. Some weekends are good. When couples go out on dates and guys want to impress girls, they stop at King's House corner and buy roses. Business is brisk when there are school graduations. Valentine's Day is probably the best single day of all, but the thirty days of June is fat season for rose sellers, for people who decorate churches for weddings will often come and buy out all the roses from the boys on the corner. October rains washed out Henry's business yesterday, he didn't even have money for food. If it wasn't that the doughnut youth got washed out too and just decided to share out his stock with everybody on the corner, Henry would have gone to sleep with nothing in his belly.

He looks at the roses. The red ones smell like crushed pimento and ginger. He wishes that something good would happen to him and just cancel out all the salt on his life. The bad luck that forced him to be hustling on the streets from the time that he was eleven years old. Soon he will be thirteen and every day he wishes that one of these people who drive up to the King's House stop light on their way to their upper St. Andrew houses would just stop and open their car door and say to him:

"Come, little youth, come live with me and my family. You can have your own room and you will never be hungry. We will send you to school and you can take care of the rose garden and make the place look nice."

But Henry doubts that anything like that is going to happen. Especially after last year when that boy killed that woman after she took him up off the street and gave him somewhere to live. When the police asked him why, why did the boy kill the only person who ever showed him any real kindness in life, the boy said she was a wicked woman because she wouldn't allow him to drive her car.

One day Henry had sold some lovely red roses to a woman and she had looked at them with admiration and said:

"Son, these are God's signature."

Henry was not sure what "signature" meant, so he waited until Professor came on to the corner to hustle some quick money. Professor used to be a university student until he started to study crack. Henry waited until he saw him come onto the corner with a big bunch of tough, stale-looking anthuriums trying to hustle a quick sale.

"Hey, Professor! Wha 'signature' mean?"

And Professor, who was sweating and shaking, whose hands were trembling like a very old man as he held the bunch of anthuriums that nobody was going to buy because the white spikes were turning brown at the tip like half-smoked cigarettes, managed to concentrate really hard, standing there with the shuddering bunch of red anthuriums, right outside the official residence of the Queen's representative.

Finally he said, "That means when you sign your name." Professor then started to laugh a thin, high cackling laugh because he was so proud that he remembered something. Proud that he was able to rescue a whole something from the mix-up in his mind. Henry did not quite understand. God sign God name as a flowers?

Henry did not quite understand, but this morning he wants to call out to the one whose signature is a bunch of roses because he is so tired of the street runnings.

Last week one of the flower-sellers, a boy named Kitchen Knife from the Swine Posse on Barbican Road, tried to sell "crack and roses" to two tourists. He had even written a kind of jingle inspired by the Neil Diamond song "Cracklin Rosie." The tourists, who were Neil Diamond fans, were outraged and wrote a letter to the newspaper. Now police have started to harass the flower sellers. Maybe the Governor General will order them to move from outside King's House altogether. What will Henry do then? King's House corner is the safest place in Kingston to hustle.

At first he is not sure how to address them, so he doesn't address the roses as anything, he just starts talking in the direction of the bucket.

"You want see my mother get a new man and she run me out of the house, say I must go and fight life for myself."

Henry tells the roses how his mother's new man hated him from the first time he saw him. Henry resembled his father and the man hated Henry's father and Henry. While his grandmother and grandfather were alive, he couldn't throw Henry out of the house because it was in Henry's grandparents' little house that he and his mother had gone to live in after Henry's father had left them to go and live with a young girl.

His grandparents had not liked the man, and his granny had read Psalms for him every day while she was alive. Henry's grandmother also threw some hard words against the man and Henry's mother, like:

"Look how this big old rusty tone man just come and eat off everything so that him drop *boof*, and this poor little half-starve boy child so light that him drop *tim*."

His grandmother kept saying:

"Can a woman's tender care cease toward the child she bear?" when Henry's mother started to spend hours at a time carefully washing and ironing the man's khaki uniform. The man was a hospital porter and Henry's mother took pride in the fact that when she washed and ironed his khaki pants they could stand up by themselves, while she was doing that, poor Henry was going to school mash-up and smelling sour as a young lime.

"Can a woman's tender care cease toward the child she bear?" His grandparents kept saying that, shortly before they died one right after the other. When Granny died, Grandpa stood at the graveside and stated, "Don't worry, my wife. I will soon join you."

And not even six months after that, he just did not wake up one morning. By Christmas of that year his mother gave Henry some money and told him to buy some starlights and balloons and to sell them at the stoplight. "Go fight life for yourself," she had said.

Just to make sure that Henry really left, the man told a big lie on him that he had stolen his watch and some money. He said he was going to call the police and let them lock him up, so Henry ran away, and that is how he came to be living on the street.

Henry is kneeling down over the bucket of roses by this time, talking down into them. The roses issue up their spice smell to him. After a while he stops talking and just takes deep breaths, filling up his lungs with the rose incense. He inhales deeply so that he starts to feel nice, light-headed and mellow. Sometimes Henry would smoke weed and drink hot stout when he went to a Stone Love dance. The combination of weed, hot stout, and certain dance-hall rhythms would make Henry feel all powerful, as if he could do anything, he could even say to one of his young shotter friends, "Lend me a gun, mi a go make two duppy, mi mother man and mi mother."

Henry waits in the shadows of the lane where his mother lives with the man in his grandparents' house. Henry has carefully dressed himself in dark clothes so that he blends in with the night. He waits for the man to come down the street in his khaki uniform. Henry smells him before he sees him;

the man smells like hospital, like deadhouse. Henry takes a deep breath and pulls himself farther into the shadows. The man does not see him. He goes past, pushes opens the gate, and steps up *bram* with his big government boots onto Henry's grandparents' veranda.

Henry sees his mother open the door and let the man into the house. Henry can see behind her into the room with his grandparents' big trunk bed. The worthless man never even brought his own bed. The man just came into their lives with one battered cardboard grip and a big blue and white enamel mug that was speckled like a booby egg. He drank half a gallon of tea out of it every morning and ate the lion's share of a loaf of hard-dough bread, leaving only the two bread ends for Henry and his mother.

"I want see him lie down dead like a dog a ground. And I want see mi mother, the wicked bitch, I want see her dead too. A dat me want."

But mostly he wants everything in his life to go back to being the way it was before the man came into their lives.

Also Henry did not want to go to prison. Whenever someone said, "Prison no make fi dog," Henry's grandfather would always say, "Only a man who never go a prison would say that."

His grandfather told Henry and his friends some things about prison that made Henry have nightmares for weeks. Henry is small for his age and thin, that is why he has to hustle where he is safe.

His grandmother used to tell him: "Henry, I warn you before I spawn you, stop smoke your grandfather cigarette butt. You will downgrow. You don't have to do everything like your grandfather."

But it was probably the things his grandfather told Henry about prison that stopped him from trying to kill the man and his mother.

After he inhaled the roses, Henry began to wonder what he could do next. He decides to peel off the stale outer petals of the roses. One particular rose catches his attention. The stem looks thin and what his grandmother would have called "mashated." It has a some thorns like the devil had bitten it and left a few of his teeth in it, but the flower, after he has stripped off the outer petals that are the colour of dried blood, looks perfectly fresh.

It is this rose that Henry lifts up and holds before him like a priest raising up a crucifix. He throws back his head, opens his mouth wide, and bites off the bloom of the struggling red rose. He holds it on his tongue for a while, and he can feel it burning inside his hot mouth like a red pepper light. He holds it in his mouth and inhales; and then he rolls it around and around on his tongue and then, after a while, he begins to bite down on it. It tastes hard and soft and like bird pepper and wet sugar at the same time. Henry chews and swallows the rose pulp slowly.

He sets about stripping off the rest of the outer "guard petals" of the roses that he will try to sell again today. He cuts the tips of the stems slantways as he holds them under the running water of the pipe outside, and he puts new water in the buckets. He drops white tablets of aspirin into the water to help revive the fading roses. The other day somebody told about putting sugar in the water. He might try reviving them with sugar tomorrow. He steps out of the room where street boys squat, carrying his bucket, hoping that the rose he swallowed is even now catching, taking root, in his life.

Bella Makes Life

HE WAS EMBARRASSED when he saw her coming toward him. He wished he could have just disappeared into the crowd and kept going as far away from Norman Manley International Airport as was possible. Bella returning. Bella come back from New York after a whole year. Bella dressed in some clothes that made her look like a checker cab. What in God's name was a big, forty-odd-year-old woman who was fat when she leave Jamaica, and get worse fat since she go to America, what was this woman doing dressed like this? Bella was wearing a stretch-to-fit black pants, over that she had on a loose-fitting yellow-and-black checked blouse, on her feet was a pair of yellow booties, in her hand was a big yellow handbag, and she had on a pair of yellow-framed glasses. See ya, Jesus! Bella no done yet, she had dyed her hair with red oxide and Jheri curls it till it shine like it grease and spray. Oh Bella, what happen to you? Joseph never ever bother take in her anklet and her big bracelets and her gold chain with a pendant, big as a name plate on a lawyer's office, marked "Material Girl."

Joseph could sense the change in Bella through her letters. When she just went to New York, she used to write him D.V. regularly every week.

Dear Joe Joe,

How keeping, my darling? I hope fine. I miss you and the children so till I think I want to die. Down in Brooklyn here where I'm living, I see a lot of Jamaicans, but I don't mix up with them. The lady who sponsor me say that a lot of the Jamaicans up here is doing wrongs and I don't want to mix up with those things as you can imagine. You know that I am only here to work some dollars to help you and me to make life when I come home. Please don't have any other woman while I'm gone. I know that a man is different from a woman, but please do try and keep yourself to yourself till we meet and I'm saving all my love for you.

Your sweet, sweet Bella

That was one of the first letters that Bella write Joseph, here one of the last letters.

Dear Joseph,

What you saying? I really sorry that my letter take so long to reach you and that the post office seem to be robbing people money left, right, and centre. Man, Jamaica is something else again. I don't write as often as I used to because I working two jobs. My night job is doing waitressing in a nightclub on Nostrand Avenue,

the work is hard but tips is good. I make friends with
a girl on the job named Yvonne and sometimes she and
I go with some other friends on a picnic or so up to Bear
Mountain. I guess that's where Peaches says she saw
me. I figure I might as well enjoy myself while I not
so old yet.

Your baby,
Bella

Enjoy herself? This time Joseph was working so hard to
send the two children to school clean and neat, Joseph become
mother and father for them, the man even learn to plait the
little girl hair. Enjoy himself? Joseph friend them start to
laugh after him because is like him done with woman.

Joseph really try to keep himself to himself, although the
nice, nice woman who live at the corner of the next road, nice
woman you know, was always talking so pleasant to him.
Joseph, make sure that the two of them just remain social
friends . . . and Bella up in New York about she gone a Bear
Mountain, make blabbamouth Peaches come back from New
York and tell everybody in the yard how she buck up Bella at
a picnic and how Bella really into the Yankee life fully.

It was Norman, Joseph's brother, who said that Bella
looked like a checker cab. Norman had driven Joseph and the
children to the airport in his van to meet Bella because she
wrote to say "she was coming with a lot of things." When
the children saw her they jumped up and down yelling,
"Mama come, Mama come." When Norman saw her (he was
famous for his wit), he said, "Blerd naught! A Bella dat,

whatta way she favour a checker cab." When Bella finally cleared her many and huge bags from Customs and came outside, Joseph was very quiet, he didn't know quite how to greet the new Bella. Mark you Bella was always "nuff," but she really was never as wild as this. She ran up to Joseph and put her arms around him. Part of him felt a great sense of relief that she was home, that Joseph and Bella and their two children were a family once more.

Bella was talking a little too loudly. "Man, I tell you those Customs people really give me a warm time, oh it's so great to be home though, it was so cold in New York!" As she said this she handed her winter coat with its mock-fur collar to her daughter, who staggered under the weight of it. Norman, who was still chuckling to himself over his checker cab joke, said, "Bwoy, Bella, a you broader than Broadway." Bella said, "Tell me about it."

They all set out for home. Joseph kind of kept quiet all the way there and allowed the children to be united with their mother . . . she was still Mama Bella, though, asking them about school, if they had received certain parcels she had sent, and raising an alarm how she had sent a pair of the latest high-top sneakers for the boy and that they had obviously stolen them at the post office.

Every now and again she leaned across and kissed Joseph. He was a little embarrassed but pleased. One time she whispered in his ear, "I hope you remember I've been saving all my love for you." This was a new Bella, though, the boldness and the forwardness was not the old Bella who used to save all her love for when they were alone together with the bolt on the door because she did not encourage too much display of affection before the children.

That change in Bella pleased Joseph. There were some other changes in Bella that did not please him so much, though. Like he thought that all the things in the many suitcases were for their family. No sir! While Bella brought quite a few things for them, she had also brought a lot of things to sell, and many evenings when Joe Joe come home from work just wanting a little peace and quiet, to eat his dinner, watch a little TV, and go to him bed and hug up his woman, his woman (Bella) was out selling clothes and "things." She would go to different offices and apartment buildings and she was always talking about which big important brown girl owed her money. Joseph never loved that. He liked the idea of having extra money, they now had a number of things they could not afford before, but he missed the old Bella who he could just sit down and reason with and talk about certain little things that a one have store up in a one heart . . . Bella said, America teach her that if you want it, you have to go for it. Joe Joe nearly ask her if she want what? The truth is that Joe Joe felt that they were doing quite all right. He owned a taxi that usually did quite well, they lived in a Government Scheme that gave you the shell of a house on a little piece of land under a scheme called "Start to build up your own home." And they had built up quite a comfortable little two-bedroom house with a nice living room, kitchen, bathroom, and veranda. What did Bella mean when she said, "You have to make it"? As far as Joe Joe was concerned, he had made it. And him was not going to go and kill himself to get to live upon Beverly Hills because anyhow the people up there see all him old friend them come up that way to visit him, them would call police and set guard dog on them! Joe Joe was fairly contented. What happen to Bella?

"Come, ya little Bella, siddown, make me ask you something. You no think say that you could just park the buying and selling little make me and you reason bout somethings?"

"Joe Joe, you live well, yah. I have three girls from the bank coming to fit some dresses and if them buy them then is good breads that."

After a while, Joe Joe stopped trying to reclaim their friendship. After a month, Bella said she wanted to go back to New York. Joe Joe asked her if she was serious.

"You know that nobody can't love you like me, Joe Joe."

Joe Joe wondered about that. Sometimes he looked at the lady at the corner of the next road, their social friendship had been severely curtailed since Bella returned home, but sometimes he found himself missing the little talks they used to have about life and things in general.

She was a very simple woman. He liked her style, she was not fussy. Sometimes he noticed a man coming to her, the man drive a Lada, look like him could work with the government, but him look married too. You know how some man just look married? Well, this man here look like a man who wear a plaid bermuda shorts with slippers when him relax on a Sunday evening, and that is a married-man uniform.

When Joe Joe begun to think of life without Bella, the lady at the corner of the next road began to look better and better to him.

"So Bella really gone back a New York?"

"Yes, my dear, she say she got to make it while she can."

"Make what?"

"It!"

"A wha it so?"

"You know . . . Oh forget it."

And that is what Joe Joe decided to do. The lady, whose name was Miss Blossom, started to send over dinner for Joe Joe not long after Bella went back to New York.

"Be careful of them stew peas and rice you a eat from that lady they you know, mine she want tie you," Peaches said. Joe Joe said, "True?" and continued eating the dinner that Miss Blossom had sent over for him. He didn't care what Peaches said, her mouth was too big anyway. He just wanted to enjoy eating the "woman food." Somehow, food taste different, taste more nourishing when a woman cook it.

Bella write to say that she was doing fine.

Dear Joe Joe,

I know you're mad with me because you didn't want me to come back to the States, but, darling, I'm just trying to make it so that you and me and the children can live a better life and stop having to box feeding outta hog mouth.

Now that really hurt Joe Joe. He would never describe their life together as that . . . True, sometimes things had been tight, but they always had enough to eat and wear. Box feeding outta hog mouth, that was the lowest level of human existence, and all these years he thought they were doing fine, that is how Bella saw their life together. Well, sir, Joe Joe was so vex that him never even bother to reply to that letter.

Joe Joe started to take Miss Blossom to pictures, and little by little the line of demarcation between social friends and sweethearts just blurred. Joe Joe tell her that the married man better stop come to her and Miss Blossom say him was only a social friend and Joe Joe say "Yes," just like how him and her was social friend . . . and she told him he was too jealous and him say: "Yes, but I don't want to see the man come to you again," and she said, "Lord, Joe Joe."

Little by little Miss Blossom started to look after the children and look after Joe Joe's clothes and meals and is like they choose to forget Bella altogether. Then one Christmastime Bella phone over the grocery shop and tell Mr. Lee to tell Joe Joe that she was coming home for Christmas.

Well to tell the truth, Joe Joe never want to hear anything like that. Although Miss Blossom couldn't compare to Bella because Bella was the first woman Joe Joe ever really love. Joe Joe was feeling quite contented and he was a simple man, him never really want to take on Bella and her excitement and her "got to make it." Anyway, him tell Miss Blossom say Bella coming home and she say to him: "Well, Joe, I think you should tell her that anything stay too long will serve two masters, or two mistresses as the case might be."

Joe Joe say: "Mmm . . . but remember say Bella is mi baby mother, you know; and no matter what is the situation, respect is due."

Miss Blossom say: "When Bella take up herself and gone to New York and leave you, she should know that respect was due to you too." Joe Joe say: "Yes, but I am a man, who believe that all things must be done decently and in good order, so if I am going to put away Bella, I have to do it in the right and proper way."

Miss Blossom say: "I hope that when Bella gone again you don't bother come ask me fi nuttin!" Joe Joe became very depressed.

If Bella looked like a checker cab the first time, she looked like *Miami Vice* this time, in a pants suit that look like it have in every colour flowers in the world and the colour them loud! And Bella broader than ever. Oh man. Norman said:

"Bees must take up Bella inna that clothes dey. Any how she pass Hope Gardens them must water her."

Bella seemed to be oblivious to the fact that Joe Joe was under great strain. She greeted him as if they had parted yesterday,

"Joe Joe, what you saying, sweet pea?"

Joe Joe just looked at her and shook his head and said:

"Wha happen, Bella?"

They went home but Joe Joe felt like he and the children went to meet a stranger at the airport. He began to wonder exactly what she was doing in America, if she really was just waitressing at that club. One night when they were in bed, Bella suggested to him that he should come forward and try some new moves because this was the age of women's liberation. Joe Joe told her that maybe she should liberate her backside outta him life because he couldn't take her.

Bella cried and said how much she loved him. Then things became really intense and it was like a movie and they had to turn up the radio really high to prevent the children from hearing them.

Joe Joe decided to just bite him tongue while Bella was home. He took to coming home very late all through the Christmas season because the house was usually full of Bella's posse, including the "Yvonne" of Bear Mountain Fame, and when they came to visit, the house was just full up of loud laughing and talking and all kinds of references that Joe Joe didn't understand. The truth was that he was really dying for Bella to leave. He really didn't much like the woman she had become. First of all everything she gave to him or the children, she tell them how much it cost . . .

"Devon, beg you don't bother to take that Walkman outside, is Twenty-Nine Ninety-Nine, I pay for it at Crazy Eddies," or,

"Ann-Marie, just take time with that jagging suit, I pay Twenty-Three Dollars for it in May's Department Store." Oh Lord!

Bella also came armed with two junior Jheri curls kits and one day Joe Joe come home and find him son and him daughter heads well Jheri curls off.

Joe Joe nearly went mad.

"So you want Devon fi turn pimp or what?"

"Joe, you really so behind time, you should see all the kids on my block."

"On your block? Well me ago black up you eye if you don't find some way fi take that nastiness outta my youth man hair. Him look like a cocaine seller. Bella, what the hell do you? You make America turn you inna idiat? Why you don't just gwan up there and stay then, me tired a you foolishness."

Bella said she couldn't believe that Joe Joe was saying this to her, then she told him that he was a worthless good-for-nuttin and that him never have no ambition, him just want to stay right inna the little two by four (their house) and no want no better and that she was really looking for a better way and that he clearly did not fit into her plans.

Joe Joe say him glad she talk what was in her mind because now him realize say that she was really just a use him fi convenience through no man a New York don't want her. Bella said. Then he said, Oh, they said some things to each other!

Bella catch her fraid though and try wash out the Jheri curls outta Devon hair. No amount of washing could bring it round. The barber had to nearly bald the little boy head and he spent the worst Christmas of his life. All his friends slapped him on the back of his head as they passed by.

Right after New Year's Day, Bella pack up herself and go straight back to New York.

Joe Joe make a two weeks pass before him make a check by Miss Blossom. The whole Christmas gone him never see her. He figured that she had gone to spend the holidays in the country with her family. When he asked in the yard where she was, they told him they had no idea where she was gone, and that her room was empty. Joe Joe felt like a beaten man. He went home and decided to just look after the children and rest within himself.

About a month later he was driving home when he saw somebody looking like Miss Blossom standing at the corner of the road. It looked like Miss Blossom, but no, it couldn't be, this woman was dressed like a punk in full black. She had on a black socks with lace frothing over the top of her black leather ankle boots. A big woman. He slowed the cab down and said:

"Blossom, where you was?" and then he thought quickly, "No, don't bother answer me, you go to New York, right?"

"No," said Blossom, "I was in Fort Lawdadale. You seem to think only Bella one can go to America."

Joe Joe never even bother ask her if she want a drive. Him just draw a gear and move off down the road, then him go inside him house and slam the door.

Before him drop asleep, it come to him that maybe what him should do was to find an American woman who wanted to live a simple life in Jamaica. Joseph know a Rasta man name Makonen who have a nice Yankee woman like that.

By Love Possessed

~

S OMETIMES SHE USED TO wake up and just look at him
lying asleep beside her, she would prop herself up on
one elbow and study his face. He slept like a child, knees
drawn up to his stomach, both hands tucked between his
thighs. His mouth was always slightly open when he slept,
and his mouth-water always left a damp patch on the pillow-
case. No matter how many days after, it seemed the patch
would always be damp, and every time she washed it she
would run her finger over the stain and her mind would pick
up the signal and move back to the image of him lying asleep.
When the radio next door began to play the first of the mor-
ning church services, she would know that it was time to
begin to get ready to go to work. From Monday to Saturday,
every day, her days began like this. She would go to the
kitchen to prepare his breakfast, then she would leave it cov-
ered up on top of the stove over a bowl of hot water. Then she
would go to the bathroom, bathe in the cold early morning
water, and then get dressed. Just before she left she always

placed some money on the top of the bureau for his rum and cigarettes, then she would say to his sleeping form, "Frenchie, ah gone, take care till I come back."

Dottie sometimes wondered how she was so lucky to be actually living with Frenchie. He was easily the best-looking man in Jones Town, maybe in the whole of Jamaica, and she, ten years older than him, tall and skinny and "dry up." She had never had luck with men and she had resigned herself to being an old maid a long time ago. She was childless, "a mule," as really unkind people would say. She worked hard and saved her money, and she kept a good house. Her two rooms in the yard were spotless. She had a trunk bed that was always made up with pretty chenille spreads, a lovely mahogany bureau, a wardrobe with good-quality glass mirrors and in the front room, in pride of place, her china cabinet. Nobody in the yard, maybe in Jones Town, maybe in the whole of Jamaica, had a china cabinet so full of beautiful things. Dottie had carefully collected them over the years and she never used them. Once a year when she was fixing up her house at Christmas, she would carefully take them out, the ware plates, cups and saucers, tureens, glasses, lemonade sets, serving dishes and teapots, and she would carefully wash them. This took her nearly a whole morning. She washed them in a pan of soapy warm water, rinsed them in cold water, then dried them with a clean towel. Then she would rearrange them artistic- ally in the cabinet. On that night, she would sometimes treat herself to a little drink of Porto Pruno wine, sitting by her- self in her little living room, and she would gaze on her china cabinet, enjoying the richness within, the pretty colours and the lights bouncing off the glasses. Her sister always said that she worshipped her possessions. Maybe she did, but what else did she have? Till she met Frenchie.

There was one other thing that Dottie really liked: she liked the movies, and that is how she met Frenchie. She was in the line outside the Ambassador Theatre one Saturday night, waiting to get into a hot triple bill, when she struck up a conversation with him. He was standing in the line behind her and she remembered feeling so pleased that a man as good-looking as this was talking to her. They moved up in the line till they got to the cashier; she, being ahead of him, took out ten shillings to pay for herself. It was the easiest most natural thing in the world for her to offer to pay for him when he suddenly raised an alarm that his pocket had been picked. If she had been seeing straight, she would have noticed that some people were laughing when he raised the alarm. But she didn't see anything except the handsome brown-skin man with "good hair," straight nose, and a mouth like a woman's.

It was the best triple bill Dottie ever watched. He had walked her home. All the way home they talked about the movie. His favourite actor was Ricardo Montalban; she liked Dolores del Rio, for that is how she would like to have looked, sultry and Spanish, for then she and Frenchie would make a striking couple, just like two movie stars. As it was, she looked something like Popeye's girlfriend Olive Oyl and he was probably better looking than Ricardo Montalban.

Frenchie did not work. He explained that he used to have a job at the wharf, but he got laid off when his back was damaged unloading some cargo. She sympathized with him and some nights she would rub the smooth expanse of his back with wintergreen oil. He said he liked how her hands felt strong. Frenchie moved in with Dottie about two weeks after they met. At first, she was a little shy about having a man in her bedroom, then she began to be very proud of it. At last she was just like any other woman in the yard. As a matter of fact, she was luckier than all of them, for Frenchie was so good-looking. "She mind him. Dottie buy down to the very drawers that Frenchie wear," said her sister, "not even a kerchief the man buy for himself."

The people in the yard would laugh at her behind her back, they wondered if Frenchie kept women with her. Winston, her nephew, said:

"Chu, rum a Frenchie woman, man, you ever see that man hug up a rum bottle?"

Now that was true. Frenchie loved rum and rum loved him, for he never seemed to get drunk. As a matter of fact, every day he spent a good eight hours, like a man going to work, in Mr. Percy's bar at the corner. After Dottie had gone to the St. Andrew house where she did domestic work for some brown people, Frenchie would wake up. He would bathe, eat the breakfast that Dottie had left for him, and get dressed, just like any man going to work. He always wore white short-sleeved shirts, which Dottie washed whiter than pelican shit; he favoured khaki pants, so she ironed both shirt and pants very carefully.

He would get dressed slowly, put some green brilliantine in his hair and brush it till it looked like a zinc fence, or as one of the men in the yard said, "Every time I see you hair, Frenchie,

I feel seasick." Frenchie would laugh, showing the gold caps on his front teeth, run his hand over his hair, and say, "Waves that behaves, bwoy, waves that behaves." When his toilette was over, he would walk leisurely up the road to the bar. The one thing that made you realize that he could not have been going to work like any other decent man was what he had on his feet. He always wore backless bedroom slippers.

Frenchie would sit in the bar and make pronouncements on matters ranging from the private life of the royal family (Princess Margaret was a favourite topic), to West Indian cricket (he always had inside knowledge on these matters), general world affairs, and, most of all, the movies.

Everybody was in awe of Frenchie, he was just so tough, handsome, and in control of life. His day at the bar usually ended at around five p.m., just like any other working man. Then he would walk home and join the domino game that went on constantly in the yard. Usually Dottie would find him at the domino table when she burst in through the gate, always in a hurry, anxious to come home and fix his dinner. She always said the same thing when she came through the gate, "Papa, ah come," and he, looking cool and aloof, eyes narrowed through the cigarette smoke, would say, "Oh, yu come."

Dottie always experienced a thrill when he said that, it was a signal of ownership, the slight menace in his voice was exciting, it gave her the right to say:

"Frenchie vex when I come home late . . ."

She would hurry to fix his dinner and set it on the table before him. She hardly ever ate with him, but sat at the table watching him eat. "Every day Frenchie eat a Sunday dinner," Winston would say. It was true, Dottie cooked only the best for Frenchie. He ate rice and peas at least three times per week, unlike everybody else who only ate it on Sundays. Dottie would leave the peas soaking overnight and half boil them in the morning so that they could finish cooking quickly when she hurried home in the evenings. He also had beef steak at least twice a week and "quality fish" and chicken the rest of the week.

Dottie lived to please Frenchie. She was a character in a film, *By Love Possessed*. Then one day in Mr. Percy's bar, the movies turned into real life. Frenchie was sitting with his usual group of drunkaready friends talking about a movie he had seen when a stranger stepped into the saloon; actually he was an ordinary man.

He had a mean and menacing countenance because he was out of work and things were bad at home. He walked into the bar and ordered a white rum and sat on a bar stool scowling, screwing up his face every time he took a sip of the pure 100% proof cane spirit, and suddenly Frenchie's incessant talking began to bother the stranger; the more Frenchie talked, the more it bothered him. The more the man looked at Frenchie's pretty-boy face and his soft-looking hands, the more he hated him.

Then Frenchie reached a high point of the story he was telling.

He was painting a vivid picture of the hero, wronged by a man who doubted his integrity, and Frenchie was really into it . . . he became the wronged hero before everyone's eyes, his voice trembled, his eyes widened in disbelief as the audience gazed spellbound at him. "Then the star boy say," said Frenchie, "him say, 'What kind of man do you think I am?'" The stranger at the bar never missed a beat . . . he replied, "A batty man." And the bar erupted. The laughter could be heard streets away. The barmaid laughed till they had to throw water on her to stop her from becoming hysterical. All the people who had ever wanted to laugh at Frenchie laughed at him. All the people who envied him his sweet-boy life laughed at him. Everybody was laughing at him.

The uproar didn't die down for almost half an hour and people who heard came running in off the streets to find out what had happened. One man took it upon himself to tell all the newcomers the story, over and over again. Frenchie was sitting stunned, he tried to regain face by muttering that the man was a blasted fool, but nobody listened.

Finally, the self-appointed raconteur went over to him and said, "Cho, Frenchie, you can't take a joke?" Then he lowered his voice, taking advantage of the fallen hero and said, "All the same yu know everybody must wonder bout you, how a good-looking man like you live with a mawgre dry up ooman like Dottie. She fava man, she so flat and crawny." Upon hearing this, Frenchie got angrier, and oddly enough, he wasn't angry at the man, he was angry at Dottie. It was true, she didn't deserve him, she was mawgre and crawny and dry up and really was not a woman that a handsome, sexy man like him should be with. No wonder the blasted ugly bwoy facety with him. He understood what the hero meant in the movies when he said he saw red. Frenchie felt like he was drowning in a sea of blood . . . he wanted to kill Dottie! He got up and walked out of the bar to go home.

When Dottie hurried in through the door that evening, saying breathlessly, "Papa, ah come," she was met with the following sight: Frenchie standing at the door of her front room with her best soup tureen in one hand and four of her best gold-rimmed tumblers stacked inside each other in the other hand, and as soon as he saw her he flung them into the street. He went back inside and emerged with more of the precious things from her china cabinet and he flung them into the street where they broke with a rich full sound on the asphalt. After a while, he developed a steady rhythm, beginning to take what looked like the same amount of steps each time he went into the house, then emerging with some crockery or glass, and walking to the edge of the veranda with the same amount of steps and with an underarm bowling action, he'd fling the precious things into the street. Dottie screamed, she ran up the steps and clutched at him; he gave her a box, which sent her flying down the steps. Everybody in the yard screamed. The men kept saying that he had gone rass, mad. Nobody tried to restrain him for he had murder in his eyes and he never stopped till he had broken all of Dottie's things and then he walked out of the yard.

"Frenchie bad no rass, bwoy. You see when him just fling the things, chuh." Frenchie's name became a great legend in the neighbourhood, nobody had ever seen anybody "mash it up" like that so; nobody had ever seen anybody in such a glorious temper "mash up the place to blow wow." Nobody remembered him for "What kind of man do you think I am?"

Even poor broken Dottie remembered him for his glorious temper. She would have forgiven him for breaking her precious things; she would like to have been able to tell the story of how bad her man was and about the day he broke everything in her china cabinet and boxed her down the steps. But he was gone, so what was the point.

Dottie kept going to the Saturday-night triple bills at the Ambassador, but she never saw Frenchie again. Eventually she took a live-in job and gave up her rooms in the yard.

Don't Sit on the Beauty Seat

SHE AND HER HUSBAND are sitting and holding hands on the bus making its way through West Vancouver to the Horseshoe Bay ferry terminal when a middle-aged woman gets on. She whispers to him:

"That woman looks like she shops at the same boutique as her teenaged daughter."

"You mean one of those stores done up in industrial grey with a one-word name like 'Paradox'?"

To the woman who bounces on to the bus in tight black jeans and a black graffitied T-shirt, she tries to signal not to sit on the beauty seat.

But no, the woman heads straight for the side seat, which in this part of the world is reserved for the handicapped. Just as Mrs. Mutton-dressed-as-lamb settles herself, and her silver chandelier earrings stop swinging, a young boy with a skateboard up under his arm scrambles on to the bus and slides a few feet down the aisle until he stands facing the middle-aged woman.

"Good on you, old lady, you shoved me down just so you could get on first, enjoy the ride."

Her husband leans over and says in a low voice:

"Clearly the last thing she is going to do now is enjoy this ride."

The beauty seat is the one the pretty young girls who wanted to call attention to themselves always headed for when they got into the Jolly Joseph, which is what Kingstonians called the buses run by the Jamaica Omnibus service. When she was young she would sometimes ignore her inner voice, but one day when she'd boarded the bus and her inner voice had said, *"Don't sit on the beauty seat,"* she'd listened and went and sat instead in a seat near the back and just then her old crush had gotten on.

The last time she'd seen him he'd been driving away from the traffic lights outside the Carib Theatre in his black Chevy with the fish fins. When he had stopped the car to let off her and her friend Brenda, he'd looked over his shoulder and smiled at her as she opened the back door to get out.

She had said:

"Thank you so much for the drive."

"My sister, it was my pleasure, I hope to see you again soon."

To Brenda he'd said:

"Catch you later, Bren."

Then as the light turned green, he'd taken a hard draw off his cigarette, hitched a gear, and sped off.

And then a year later, there he was, riding a bus she was on, dressed in khaki shirt and pants and wearing a black beret decorated with a pin in the shape of a fist emblazoned with the letters RRM in red.

One wouldn't say he was dirty, but he who used to look as if the maid had spent the morning ironing his white long-sleeved arrow shirt, which he always wore with the sleeves folded back just so, just above his wrists, could have bene-fited from somebody's laundering skills. As he seated him-self in the very back of the bus, she who had spent a good part of her last summer's school holidays praying for him to call her, began to pray that he would not recognize her, for surely her new finished-with-school look would cause him to call her "*Decadent materialistic Jezebel*!"

He proceeded to take out a *Gleaner* newspaper from the battered duffle bag stamped with the silhouette of a rampant Puma that he'd dropped at his feet. He held the paper right up close to his bloodshot eyes. What happened to his glasses? That's one of the things she'd liked about him; his tortoise-shell glasses made him look like a thinker. Word around the sixth form association had been that he was going to go away to university to study political science.

She remembered when she first saw him at the Sixth Form Association debate. "The topic of this debate is: Heights by great men reached and kept were not attained by sudden flight, but they, while their companions slept were toiling upwards through the night: true or false?"

"Madame Chairman, I wish," said Mercutio Brown, the

captain of the Calabar Boys School debating team, "to eluci-
date upon the fallacies of my neophyte colleagues."

That had brought the house down; and for three straight
minutes, Madame Chairman, who was a very bossy girl from
St. Andrew High School, was unable to control the two hun-
dred and fifty or so boisterous sixth formers in the audience.
From left of the stage where he, as captain of the St. Georges
College debating team, had been standing looking impatient
and annoyed while the audience laughed at Mercutio a.k.a.
swallow-the-dictionary Brown's verbosity, he had ignored
all protocol and launched in:

"I'm here to say to you, members of the Jamaica Sixth
Form Association, that a) All of this that we are engaged in
here is a tired old colonial business and b) If we must have
these debates, then let us at least choose some more relevant
topics and c) to say that, not only is the topic of this debate
a particularly stale old maxim, it is also a false one. It is
patently, blatantly false. Why? Because the majority of our
people have been toiling upwards, downwards, crossways,
and always, morning, noon, and night, for nearly four hun-
dred years, and the overwhelming majority of our people
will never reach nor keep any heights, great or otherwise,
because of this neo-colonial system that is keeping us down
in this country!" That is as far as he had gotten before the
English teacher from St. Hugh's, where the debate was being
held, had gone up on stage, taken over the mike, and declared
the debate suspended. She even suspended the "social" that
was to have taken place after the debate. This caused some of
the girls who boarded at all girls' schools – young ladies who

hardly ever saw a man, except raddled ancient handymen and gardeners specially recruited to work at all girls' boarding schools from the employment agency of Not Lady Chatterly's Mellors – to burst into tears. Several of these cloistered young ladies who had been looking forward to outrageous flirtations and surreptitious feel-ups from the fit young men of Kingston College, Jamaica College, St. Georges College, Calabar, Wolmers, and Excelsior College wept openly as they filed onto their various schoolbuses.

She and her friend Brenda were not boarders. They had decided that since the social was cancelled they might as well go to a movie. As they walked out to the bus stop, he'd driven up in the big black Chevy with the fish fins and offered them a ride.

Brenda's grandfather was one of the four leftists who had been expelled from the People's National Party in the 1950s for holding extreme socialist views. Once, Brenda had brought her grandfather's copy of Mao's *Little Red Book* to school. She'd wrapped it in her gym shorts, and after school she had invited a few of them to a viewing down by the exact spot beside the tennis courts where the Christian girls met every Friday afternoon to sing hymns and testify how they had given themselves to the Lord, as opposed to giving themselves to the boys of Kingston College. The book was little and it was red and it was written in Chinese script that one of the girls said made it look like a book full of Peaka Pow tickets, Peaka Pow being the Chinese gambling game that people all over the city of Kingston used to play on a daily basis.

As Brenda sat down beside him in the front seat of the big black Chevy, she'd said:

"Hey, Fidel Junior, you're happy that you mashed up the debate?"

Instead of answering Brenda, he'd turned around and said to her as she settled herself in the backseat: "What is such a sweet-looking young lady like you doing keeping company with my friend, Comrade Brenda? Don't let her lead you astray, you know."

Brenda had said:

"Look who is talking about leading people astray! You know it's because of you why they cancelled the social, they're going to expel you from school one of these days."

"I'm looking forward to that, it will look good on my C.V. when I become the prime minister of Jamaica."

Brenda and he had both gone to the same expensive kindergarten as children, and for the rest of the ride the two of them had exchanged news about their mutual friends while she sat silent in the backseat.

He'd dropped them off outside the Carib Theatre, and she and Brenda went to a four o'clock matinee. While they waited for the show to start, Brenda told her about him. He had been born in Cuba and had been brought to Jamaica as a baby when his parents fled from Fidel Castro.

"Get this," Brenda said. "His parents owned a big tobacco plantation in Cuba and they managed to get out most of their money before 1959. They're filthy rich. They support this group of Cubans in Miami who are always plotting how to assassinate Castro."

"So how come he's so radical?"

"He hates his parents. He says they treat their Alsatian dogs better than they treat the maid and the gardener and all they care about is money. Plus I think he's really close to some of those Jesuit priests at his school who are into what they call *liberation theology*. I wouldn't be surprised if he joined the priesthood, that is one guy who just moves mystically, nobody can really figure him out."

"I wonder if he likes me, he said he'd hoped he see me again."

Later that evening after she got home, Brenda telephoned and said:

"He likes you. I called him and accused him of lusting after you and that I saw him checking you out in the rearview mirror. He said what he liked about you is how you looked righteous."

She kept hoping that Brenda had given him her phone number and that he would call, but he never did.

Then one day, some time later, Brenda told her she'd heard that he'd joined an ultra-radical left-wing organization called RRM for Radical Righteousness Movement and that their philosophy was a bizarre mixture of extreme Marxism-Leninism combined with Old Testament blood-and-fire teachings. Brenda said he'd just turned his back and walked away from his family's many-roomed mansion with a maid to wash, and one to cook, and a housekeeper, and a school girl to assist the laundress and the cook and be there for the son to practise on, and a gardener and a yard boy who was the one they said introduced him to the wisdom weed that smoked out a hive of wasps in his head.

An older woman who was sitting on the beauty seat had called down the aisle of the Jolly Joseph:

"So what happen, comrade, when the revolution come you going take away one of the two cow that my neighbour have and give me one?"

Her old crush had let the newspaper fall to the floor as he started to curse.

"Firebun all lumpen!" That is how his Jeremiad began. "Brimstone, blood, and fire for you, you ignorant running dog of Babylon."

He cursed, no, he blooded the upstart questioner sitting on the beauty seat, blooded her in an almost seamless combination of Marxist rhetoric and Old Testament curses. He'd berated the woman from the time it took the bus to travel from King Street to Cross Roads, at which point the mortified questioner jumped up off the beauty seat and fled from the bus, muttering to herself, "It was only a little joke . . . only a little joke."

Her old crush never did acknowledge her that day on the Jolly Joseph bus in Kingston as she sat cringing in her window seat, not daring to stand up and expose her hot-pink lips and miniskirt to his gorgon gaze. She waited till he'd disembarked before she got off at the next stop. Even though she'd planned to get off at Liguanea Plaza and go to browse in

Readers Bookstore, she just sat there praying he would not recognize her as the bus wheezed past her stop. She did not move from her seat until after he'd raised himself up like the puma on his duffle bag, which he hoisted up over his shoulder and stepped off the bus.

On the bus, which is headed for the Horseshoe Bay terminal, all is quiet after the skateboarder has shamed the middle-aged woman who moves to another seat, then gets off just two stops after she boarded the bus. She says to her husband:

"Remind me to tell you a story about seeing somebody on a bus in Kingston one day."

"One of your old boyfriends?"

"Not quite, but it's kind of an interesting story, I'll tell you about it when we get home."

He squeezes her hand and they move closer to each other as the bus speeds up.

God's Help

S YLVIE, WHO WAS SITTING on one of the three chairs
George had bought for their small room, folded her
hands over her belly, which rose full before her from her
lap. Thoughts of lying-in fee, baby clothes, rent money,
food money, lawyer money were chasing round and round
in her brain, kicking up something like a dust cloud of
anxiety filling up her whole head. She didn't hear when
her cousin Gatta, who had come to visit Sylvie only to
hear the dreadful news about what happened to poor
George, said:

"Listen to me, Sylvie, every week down at Brother Sam
Church, them give out some box of food from foreign.
Sometime them give away clothes and things from foreign
too, so you might all get some baby things."

"Yes, but what me have to do to get that?"

"Nothing, you just join the church and go every now
and again."

"But, Gatta, mi no have no church frock can fit mi, you don't see how mi get big quick, and furthermore, even if me can find a frock, I don't have no hat fi wear."

"Lawd, missis, nobody don't wear hat go a church again."

"That a inna town, me no fully used to town ways yet . . . but Lord what I going to do though, eh?"

Sylvie didn't really like this plan Gatta had come up with to help her out after she told her what happened to George. In the country where she came from, Sylvie went to church every Sunday, willingly. As a matter of fact, she loved going to church and she really didn't feel sure that what Gatta was suggesting they do was not some kind of sin – she wasn't sure what sin it was – but it didn't sound right to her. To just go and join a church so you could get food and maybe some used clothes. You should join a church because you wanted to go there and worship God, at least that is what Sylvie believed.

"Boy, just through circumstances eh, just through a person can't do any better."

Up until four months ago Sylvie was an extremely contented woman. She and George living so good in their little room in the big yard. The room was like a palace to Sylvie. They had a bed, a dresser, and a little table and three chairs. "One fi visitor," George had said. They also had a radio, and Sylvie had planted mint and thyme and basil in paint pans that she had set outside the window. Sometimes in the before day morning, when a cool breeze from the sea passed through, she could smell the mint and the thyme and she imagined that she was back in the country.

Many people had said that Sylvie had no ambition.

She was such a pretty girl with her smooth sambo colouring and her dark ackee seed eyes, Sylvie with the black gums and the pretty teeth, only one thing though, her head dry, which meant that no matter how hard she tried, her hair just wouldn't grow thick and long. She had been so glad when low afros came into style and George said, "But, Sylvie, you was always my soul girl."

People always said that Sylvie could have gotten somebody who was much better than George. Big, black, handsome, good-hearted George. George's head was not made to take education, so it was clear to everyone that he was not going to go far because he had neither the brains nor an aptitude for wrongdoing. But Sylvie's "mind" – which is what some people would refer to as her intuition – just tell her that George was the man for her. Her soul and his just rest easy among one another. Sylvie trusted George and George trusted Sylvie, and he knew how to make her laugh and to anticipate her needs, and she did the same thing for him, and they both wanted the same thing: some children and a farm in the country because anything George put his hand to it grow. George had to leave the country and come to town, though, because he just couldn't get a start. He wanted to lease a piece of land, so he figured if he could come to town and work and save some money, one day soon they could "make life." So George went to Kingston to live with his aunt till he found a job working in the Botanical Gardens.

Sylvie lived in misery till he sent for her. He sent a message by bus driver (George not too into the writing business) to say he had paid her fare, he had rented a room, and would she just come and join him. Sylvie felt in her mind and soul that this was the right thing to do, so she went to join George in Kingston.

The bus stopped at Haywood Street Market, and Sylvie became quite frightened when she saw all the cars and buses and trucks and handcarts and what seemed like thousands of people in the streets. There were more people in this one street than there were in her entire village. Sylvie looked through the bus window anxiously for signs of George, and there standing up right beside a coconut cart she saw him, in a nice shirt that she had never seen before, and her mind and her heart just went out across the congested market square to him. She felt sure she had done the right thing by coming to join him. George greeted her by holding her around her waist.

"Come here, fat girl, make we make haste and go home, I just dying to romance you."

"Shhh, George, mind people hear!"

"Make them hear no, me no care. You hear that Sylvie, me come a town come turn deejay you know, I going cut a record, how this sound?

"Make them hear, for me no care,
"mi say is you mi really check for mi dear . . . gwan!"

And Sylvie was laughing and laughing at the sight of George, who had put down her suitcase in the middle of the street and was skanking like a man who felt that life was fine. A man in love, with his love close at hand. A man with a quiet place to go to and all the time in the world.

When she woke up next morning Sylvie tried to figure out where she was, the room was so unfamiliar. George was not in the bed, he was sitting quietly over by the table by the window. "Mi did fraid you wouldn't wake up."

"So what you think mi did dead?"

"All right no mine. Come eat, I make breakfast fi you, but since is dinnertime now you better eat you dinner too."

He looked at her so tenderly, then he said, "Sylvie, fun and joke aside, mi glad you come fi stay with me. Mi glad you come fi stay with me."

Sylvie turned to Gatta.

"Oh God, if George was here now, you see . . ."

"It don't make no sense you fret bout George now, where him is, him can't help you."

"George in the lockup," Sylvie had told Gatta. "Police lock up George, police flying squad move through the area and pick up nearly fifty people! George was standing on the sidewalk drinking a beer and them just scrape him up with everybody. Them say them holding him for questioning, say him look like a criminal bwoy name Country who wanted for robbery with aggravation." George of all people, robbery with aggravation! George in a central lockup without bail. Sylvie told Gatta how she had heard that sometimes a man could spend all two years in a lockup before the police charged him.

"Lord Jesus have mercy," Gatta said. "You know what go on inna them place dey? You know George real crime? Him poor and him no know no politician."

Sylvie told her how she had been going down to Central Police Station nearly every day to see George. The women in the yard were well acquainted with the prison runnings so they told her what to do. When she saw George in the lockup he'd told her to go back to the country, but she told him that she was not leaving.

"I not leaving you, George, I dead before I leave you."

Besides, she was seven months' pregnant.

"Come go with me Sunday," said Gatta.

Sylvie thought about it and thought about it, what choice did she have? Up until recently she had a few days domestic work, but the bigger her belly grew the more difficult work became. She just did not feel so good about going to church in the hope of getting some food and some old clothes, but what choice did she have?

"All right, Gatta, it look like I haffi go wid you."

Sylvie could not bring herself to go into church without a hat. So she'd tied her head with a clean, pretty headscarf and put on her best maternity dress, which by now was too tight for her. The hem rode up in front hoisted by her belly, and she was very uncomfortable as the zip could barely close up in the back. She took her Bible, and the few dollars that she had left to pay her bus fare, and she went with Gatta down to the Hallelujah Temple, a big concrete church that looked like a dove with wings outstretched and praying hands at the same time. They were early, and Gatta walked right down to the front of the church and made to sit down. "No, Gatta, make we sit down in the back."

"Then how them going see we, if we sit down in the back?" Reluctantly, Sylvie sat in the front row and she just felt so out of place and so conspicuous.

The members of the congregation began to file in and fill up the seats; they were mostly very well-dressed people. Sylvie's unease started to grow, she started thinking about her little church in the country where everybody knew everybody else. She wished she was back in the country right now, she and George. Sylvie began to rock back and forth as she thought about George, clasping her belly bottom, for that was where she felt all her grief. Sylvie was rocking back and forth when Gatta hissed, "Sylvie, is what wrong with you!"

Sylvie stopped and tried to sit still, her shoulders hunched over in some sort of attempt to look inconspicuous.

The service was about to begin. Reverend Samuel was preceded into the church by the choir singing in good voice. He was accompanied by two visiting foreign evangelists.

Reverend Sam welcomed the visiting evangelists and informed the church that they had come to hold a crusade. He said he hoped everyone would come to hear the words of God as spoken by these ambassadors for truth and democracy (he pronounced it *demo-crassy*). The visiting preachers stood up and brought greetings from the church overseas and said how glad they were to be visiting this beautiful island where the people were so in need of God's words.

When it was time to pray, Sylvie could not kneel as her dress was too tight. As it was binding her across her stomach, she stayed hunched over, hoping that the fact that she was not kneeling was not too obvious. The service proceeded and Sylvie did not know why, but even when she closed her eyes to pray she felt conspicuous. At some point she began to feel that Reverend Sam was staring at her. Of course when she opened her eyes he was looking straight ahead of him.

When it was time for the sermon, Reverend Sam ascended to the pulpit. He paused dramatically and clutched the sides of the lectern and he began to preach in a voice that was harsh and loud. He started off his sermon with a personal testimony of how he had been called by God to serve at a young age and how he had been preaching the gospel of repentance to sinners ever since the day he answered that call.

Reverend Samuel was a brown-skinned man of medium height with a large head and a high, sloping forehead. Gatta told her that his detractors called him More Face to Wash than Hair to Comb behind his back. He told how as a boy of twelve, although he was very bright, he had had to leave school to go and sell the *Star* newspaper on the streets of Kingston to help feed him and his mother and his five younger brothers and sisters. He preached about the day he had tried to sell a newspaper to an older man dressed in a black shirt with a round white collar who had stopped at the traffic light in a little old convertible Morris Minor.

"'Nebuchadnezzar, King of Babylon, make up him bed in a sardine can,'" the young boy was singing under his breath as he approached the little black car that had a bumper sticker with a drawing of a fish on it, and when he looked carefully he could see that the word *Jesus* filled up the body of the fish.

"No thank you, sonny, that scandal sheet is not for all like me, but I have a paper for you and it costs nothing."

And the man had handed the young Sam a flyer advertising a revival service at a church on Waltham Park Road that weekend. The boy's eyes were drawn to just one word on the flyer: *refreshments*.

The reverend painted the picture of his young self making his way, dressed in his khaki school uniform, to the revival meeting that Sunday. He told how as he'd sat on one of the long wooden benches listening to the minister who was the man in the sardine tin car, he'd imagined to himself just how he would deliver the message if it were him up there standing at that little wooden pulpit at the far end of the shabby canvas tent.

He had stayed behind and helped to pick up litter and stack up the wooden benches after the service ended, and the minister had told his wife to give the young boy some of the fried fish and hard dough bread that had been provided to attract people to the revival. The minister also told him that if he wanted, he could come back and help him again the next week and the young Samuel, whose belly was always muttering and grumbling how it wanted more food, was glad to go back and help the minister every week after that and to stay for refreshments. And that, he told the congregation, is how he began with the church.

When the old minister's eyesight started to fail, he began to call upon Samuel to come up to the pulpit and read from the Bible for him so he could then expound upon the text. By then he said the tent had grown into the large, impressive building it now was. When the old minister died, Sam, who had been honing his flamboyant preaching style from the first time he came to the church drawn by the promise of refreshments, took his place.

Reverend Sam then moved into the body of his sermon, which was titled "God helps those who help themselves." He explained that it was a sermon that was in keeping with a speech made by a prominent politician that same week about the dangers of a welfare state. The speech said that people were not to be encouraged to look to others for charity or to the state for handouts, that they were to pull themselves up by their bootstraps.

"It has come to me, brothers and sisters, that some people don't seem to want to help themselves, and even the smallest child know that God helps those who help themselves," preached Reverend Sam.

When he said those words, Sylvie felt a burning begin in her body; it started in her ears and spread across her face and moved down till it seemed to settle in her belly.

The reverend continued:

"Take this business of having children without a plan."

Sylvie just knew he was looking at her right at this point, she just knew it.

"Some of us brothers and sisters don't even think about how we are going to feed and clothe these young ones before we bring them into the world, not a thought do we give for them, we just think of our own pleasure."

Now Sylvie began to feel that all eyes in the church were directed at her belly. Sylvie sat there feeling embarrassed that she had allowed Gatta to force her to go against her feelings. She knew she should not have come to this place. Sylvie began to feel ashamed, but she was also feeling angry. Angry with herself because she had not followed her mind.

"Sylvie, you must follow your mind, woman especially must follow them mind."

She had grown up with her grandmother always saying those words to her.

Well right now, Sylvie's mind was telling her to walk out of this church.

For no matter how bad things were with her, she could still see the lack of true generosity in Reverend Sam's sermon. After all, everybody's circumstances were different. It was true that God helped those who helped themselves, but because God was God, shouldn't God help those who could not help themselves?

Reverend Sam then declared that because he was a man of God, he was still going to give to the needy at this point in the proceedings, and that he was asking the needy not to leave directly after they received their food and clothes parcels, but that they should stay behind to confess their sins and receive counselling on how to gain God's favour.

The rebuff within the sermon seemed to have gone over Gatta's head because she jumped up quickly when it was announced that the needy should stand in line.

"Come on, Sylvie."

"I not joining no line."

"What you mean!?"

"I say I not going!"

People started to stare at Gatta and Sylvie. In order to avoid making a scene, Sylvie got up and joined the line with Gatta, but by then she knew exactly what she was going to do.

Assisted by the two visiting evangelists, Reverend Sam was handing out food boxes and clothing parcels to a long line of the needy. He presented these gifts, first the food box, then the clothing parcel with whispered exhortations to the needy. The needy accepted the boxes and parcels with loud and grateful thanks.

When it came to Sylvie's turn, just as she suspected, Reverend Sam was waiting for her.

For as he stretched out his hands containing the food box, he did not whisper but declared loudly:

"Remember, sister, God helps those who help themselves!"

In response, Sylvie shook her head and said loudly:

"I don't want it."

In order not to create a scene, Reverend Sam turned to the needy directly behind Sylvie, who brushed past him. Looking neither left nor right she moved down the long carpeted aisle and straight out through the ornate double doors, out of the Hallelujah Temple. She walked down the pathway leading from the church and stepped out on to the sidewalk, crossed the street, and sat down for a while inside the bus shelter that was situated directly across from the church.

When the bus came up, she let it pass as she'd decided that she would walk home instead and use what money she had to buy a dozen green bananas and a bundle of callaloo. After a while she got to her feet and adjusted her headtie, which had slipped to the side when she'd walked so resolutely away from Reverend Sam's graceless, grudging charity. She stood up, placed one palm flat at the small of her back to brace herself, cupped her other hand under her belly, and began to move confidently and deliberately in the direction of home. While she was sitting in the bus shelter, her mind had told her that George was even now walking home too, released from lockup, in need of a good bath and a hot meal. Somehow it was all going to work out.

House Colour

⁓

From the minute she'd driven up to the guard house of the gated community with the huge expensive houses, she knew she was going to feel irritable and out of place in the company of the people a friend of hers called "DBPD – de brown people dem." Wealthy, light-skinned Jamaicans who lived in mansions like this one that had three separate living rooms and two different dining rooms and a swimming pool, but who probably paid their domestic helpers minimum wage and forbade them to eat from the same plates and drink from the same glasses they did.

Years before, an Englishman she had worked with at an advertising agency had described her at "bolshy," and that is exactly how she was feeling as she squeezed her small yellow car into the space between a Mercedes-Benz and a Range Rover. She checked her makeup in the rear-view mirror to make sure there was no lipstick on her front teeth, then she got out of the car and adjusted the floating layers of her red dress made from handkerchief linen. She'd spent way too much on it at Samantha's Boutique in the lobby of the Pegasus Hotel, and that was another reason she was feeling irritable, she knew she would not be able to write off the dress as a business expense, but she also knew she could hardly show up at a party like this in her painter's jeans and T-shirt.

As she made her way into the Christmas party being held on the manicured grounds of the home of the director of the public relations firm for which she did freelance work, she was reminding herself that this was business. That the only way she could afford to live in her charming ivy-covered cottage in the foothills of the Blue Mountains was to have a regular supply of freelance design work. So as she walked into the party she was telling herself, Smile and be sociable so you'll get more design work this coming year. Smile and slip out of yourself as much as possible when you have to stand there and pretend to be listening intently to boring people going on and on about their boring lives. Mingle, girl, mingle. But first stop off at the lavish buffet set up around the pool and fortify yourself.

"My dear, great to see you, come and meet the client you did the layout for."

Just as she'd lifted a thin wooden skewer with pieces of jerk chicken impaled on it up to her mouth, one of the directors of the agency rushed up to her with the overly handsome man in tow.

"I'll leave you two to get to know each other," said the director as she rushed off to effusively welcome another guest.

"Don't worry," he'd said. "I hate these things too."

"Why do you think I don't like being here?"

"You looked like you were going to plunge that chicken skewer into your chest when you realized that she was expecting you to babysit me."

That had made her laugh.

"I recommend the jerk chicken, but I'd avoid the meatballs. You could play ping-pong with them easily."

That had made him laugh.

"Look, I might as well tell you now, I think you are the most gorgeous woman here."

She'd ended up sharing a table with the too-handsome man.

She told herself it must have been all the imported wine passed round on trays by waiters in red shirts and black trousers that made her so open with this man who was not her usual fellow starving-artist type. When he'd got up to go, the man who, one of her socialist friends would have said, looked like he ate a plate of money for breakfast every day, asked her for her phone number and she'd written it on a festive paper napkin and handed it to him. As she was carefully wending her way home later that night in her small yellow car, she was wondering, Why did I give him my number?

But when he called early in January and invited her out to dinner, she'd said yes, and now here it was things had progressed to the point where she had actually invited him up to her small artist's cottage where he had to duck to come in the front door.

He driven up in a high-powered German vehicle. He was dressed in a light flannel shirt, designer jeans, and very expensive-looking sneakers. He was a big man, with a moustache; he had a Latin lover look, like an old-time movie star. She thought him too handsome. He said on the telephone:

"I'm coming to get you, bring a wrap or a jacket, we're going for a drive up into the mountains."

She liked going up into the mountains. The higher you climbed, the more the vegetation became interesting: all sorts of temperate-looking flowers in muted colours, feathery inflorescence, and insects not seen below where it was too hot for them to live. Once she'd been buzzed by an iridescent green bug with cellophane-like wings piped in darker green so the wings looked like window panes. Driving up into the mountains it got cooler the higher you went, and you could almost imagine you were going for a drive in some foreign country, like you were in a novel where there were lines like: *Toward evening they drove into an inn for supper.*

Once they were seated in the big car with the real-leather upholstered seats, he began to talk. He talked as if he had stored up everything he had to tell her for a long time, like he was just waiting to see her, to press his release button . . . she realized that all she had to do was to sit there and maybe say *mmmm* every now and again.

When she realized this, she did what she could do so very well. She slipped out of herself and hoisted herself up on to the roof of the car. It was a great advance view from up there. She could see way ahead of him into the oncoming distance, see the scoops in the road, the rises approaching, and into the rooms of houses; also the wind filled her hair like whispers and she laughed out loud and rolled from side to side every time the car dipped into a hollow. She thought about sitting right up on the hood, right where the silver emblem rode flagship. At best, she thought, it was a peace symbol within a circle, but peace should go with freedom and ought not be contained in a circle so she then decided she was better off upon the roof of the car. Eventually it was time to go back into herself, so she wiggled carefully through the window and re-entered, just in time, for he said just then:

"So how have you been?"

She smiled. He took that for an answer and then he continued:

"Anyway, there is a farm up ahead, it's two hundred acres and I'm planning to buy eighty more." The big car cleared the gateway and hummed to a stop inside the yard. There were about ten men standing in the driveway waiting for him. They all greeted him by crowding around the car saying, "Good evening, boss" over and over. She watched him turn into Landowner right before her eyes. He used a harsh, condescending tone when he spoke to the workers. He may have thought that he was sounding firm and authoritative, but to her he was coming across as a bully.

He didn't introduce her to the workers and she stood slightly apart, wondering what to do with herself. She decided to sit on an ornate white garden bench out in the yard and from there to slip out of herself and go walking around the garden. She turned the corner away from where he was grilling the workers about the progress of the money trees.

"Why the hell don't you do as I tell you? What's wrong with you damn people?"

There it was. "You people." DBPD always said things like "you people" when they were talking down to dark-skinned Jamaicans.

She noticed a pregnant cat lying on its side under an azalea bush. The cat was resting like a fallen-from-grace beauty queen, her belly high with kittens. It was a touching and lovely sight but what was more exciting was that the azalea bush, shading the cat, was not alone.

It was part of a whole hedge. As a matter of fact, the entire yard was bordered by azalea bushes. Can you imagine how glorious that was going to be when they bloomed? There are few things lovelier than azaleas in a day pot shimmering. He couldn't be so bad after all if he had the good taste to have a yard bordered by azaleas.

She felt that it was time to return. She was right, for as she got back to herself he said:

"It's a good thing you are such a dreamer. Come, let's go into the house."

She followed him as he took her on a tour of a house, which was decorated just right (for some people). But she kept looking around for some spare love lying accidentally somewhere, a kiss left languidly on a smooth surface. She didn't see any. And then there was this magnificent candleholder containing clean candles. And she couldn't help herself, she said:

"I like candles that have burnt, you know? Candles with dripped wings at the sides."

He said:

"What?"

They sit in the living room, there is a fireplace and she sits close to it . . . her seat is also near the door.

He sits or rather half-lies across a couch, the upholstery of which complements his shirt very well and he just looks very handsome, half-lying on that couch.

Then he speaks. He gives her warning that he is about to speak and then he says, "Please don't say anything until I have finished."

So she lets him speak. He explains that he finds himself thinking about her a lot at the most inconvenient times and things she said at their first meeting linger in his mind. The truth is he doesn't really have much time in his life for "something like this" but he wants it. He is an important person, he can afford a lot of things. She looks sleepy. He quickly says, "Anyway you get the point of what I'm saying." He says he knows he can't buy something like what he feels with her. He knows, but right now, is there anything that she needs? Can he get her anything? And she says, "Yes, azaleas." And he says, "What do you mean, azaleas?" And she says, "Do you know that your whole yard is bordered by an azalea hedge? That's wonderful! And maybe when they bloom, you could bring me some azaleas, you know, like a whole lot of them. Maybe?"

"What the hell do you mean? I'm trying to be serious, can't you be serious for once. You drive a ten-year-old car and you live in a house that can best be described as charming but ramshackle. You probably don't own it and it's a good thing you have all that ivy growing on the walls because that is all that is holding the place together, and you are asking me for azaleas?"

She says, "Yes."

He says, "I always get what I want, you know."

She says, "You probably do. Now can you take me home? I want to go home before it's dark."

On the way down, he drives very fast so she thinks it's not wise to slip outside and sit on the roof. He turns the radio on, they are playing some really whitebread anonymous music. He doesn't speak. She wonders if she should tell him about the woman with the velvet box, but he has turned up the air conditioning and air is striping out of the vents in icy waves so that every time she opens her mouth, her teeth ache.

She'd seen the woman when she went into the Swiss jewellery store to pick up her mother's watch. She herself never wears a watch and that is another thing he finds really puzzling about her.

"How can you not wear a watch? How do you know when to do what?"

"I just know," she'd said to him.

The woman had been perched on a high stool, and she was gazing down at the contents of a display case of gold chains and pendants. She looked somewhat like a crane bowing to drink from a clear pool. She also had the strangest complexion; she had what Jamaicans call "house colour," that is, she looked as if she spent most of her life indoors.

She had house colour, but she was very toned and fit-looking, very manicured and pedicured. Her hair was dyed red and styled in a beauty-queen upsweep with wispy bangs floating across her forehead. Somebody had spent a long time ironing the beige linen dress she was wearing. Someone had stood up at a crossed-legged ironing board and used up a whole can of spray starch on that dress, ironed it until it was the texture of construction paper. The woman was half-standing with her bottom just resting on the edge of the seat of the stool, her pelvis thrust forward in an oddly sexual way, her long toes gripped the front of her open-toed red mules.

The saleswoman had come hurrying through the swing doors that separated the showroom from the workroom, she was out of breath and bearing a black velvet coffer. "I'll be with you in a moment," she called out.

"It's all right, I have time. I'm just here to pick up a watch."

The saleswoman went over to the woman with house colour and gingerly placed the box before her. The woman looked up from the display of chains and pendants, then lovingly stroked the nap of the velvet box.

If she were telling him about the woman she would have said something like:

"I swear it was like something out of *Arabian Nights*. She opened the box, it was just gold! pearls! diamonds! gems! precious stones! I mean, jewellery for days! and then for the next half an hour she sits there and counts every piece. She had this little red-covered notebook and she kept checking the things in the box against the list in her book."

"I'll be with you in a moment," called the anxious saleslady.

"It's okay. I'm not really in a hurry." By this time she'd taken a seat on one of the long-legged stools in the store so she could watch, fascinated, as the woman with the velvet box counted her jewellery.

As she counted, she fired questions at the saleslady.

"What about the clasp? Are you sure the clasp on the pearls is working now? It opened up the last time I wore it, you know that I could sue you if I'd lost them?"

"Are you sure they cleaned this topaz ring? It's a druzy topaz, you know, and if they cleaned it, then why it still look like this? I don't understand why this still looks so tarnished."

Finally she shuts the lid of the velvet box and locks it with a small gold key, which is one of about ten hanging from a silver key ring that looks like it could have been a small girl's bangle.

The woman then raises the box to her bosom and cradles it like a square high baby. The store manager orders the armed security guard to escort the lady to her car.

If she were telling him the story, she would have said:

"I could just picture her driving home: sitting on the edge of her car seat, steering with one hand and holding the box to her chest with the other hand, all the while still trying hard not to crush her linen dress."

"Sorry about the wait," says the salesclerk, "but every year Miss Lady brings in that box full of jewellery, and you hear what I had to put up with."

The saleswoman sighs. If she were telling the too-handsome man this, she would have said that she'd bet him or anyone else $10,000 (which she didn't have) that the diamond tennis bracelet the woman had held up to the fluorescent light in the store had been given to her on New Year's Eve eve. Granted, the man who'd given it to her did slip away, pleading a bladder overfull at forty minutes after midnight to call and wish her Happy New Year while Byron Lee's band pumped out an extended jump-up version of "Auld Lang Syne" in the background. And because there was a photograph of him and his wife locked down in a loving embrace among the New Year's Eve revellers featured in the newspaper, he had also given her the druzy topaz ring. One New Year's Eve eve before that, the woman had taken an overdose of Valium and after she'd had her stomach pumped he'd given her those pearls, slipped the slim, flat, satin-covered box into her hand as she lay there, almost as pale as the sheets on the hospital bed. He calls upon her at all odd hours of day or night so she'd better be there every time he visits or telephones the apartment for which he pays the rent; hence her house colour. But every year, once a year, she takes that box to the jewellers and has everything in it cleaned and appraised.

In the car, a song that she recognizes comes over the radio. It's an obscure song from a Broadway musical that she happens to like, and she starts to sing along to it. She sings as if she is all by herself. She has been known to do that sometimes when she feels she has nothing more to say to somebody. Some people have found this appalling and they have said so. When the car pulls up to her gate, he shuts off the engine and says:

"Do you often do that? Just start singing out loud to yourself?"

"This is not going to work."

"I know. You are just too weird, but for some reason that just makes me want to –"

"To jump my bones?"

"If that means sleep with you . . . then yes."

"That is not going to happen."

"I guess not. Is it because you think I'm trying to buy you?"

"Yes, but that is not the only thing. Look, I might as well tell you . . ."

This is where she should tell him about the woman with the house colour in the jewellery store, she thinks, but really that is going to take too much time. If she decides to tell him about the woman, she's going to have to keep sitting in what she now thinks of as his cold-arse car, and there is no way on earth that she is going to invite him back inside her cottage after he has called it "ramshackle."

"I really hated the way you were handling those people who work for you. And the way I see it is, if I let you buy me things, one day you just might start speaking to me just like you were speaking to them, for you'll be thinking of me as one your employees."

"That is utterly ridiculous and if I had the time I'd convince you otherwise. You'd see just how I'd lay siege to your life till you surrendered to me. But here's my situation. I'm going to be extremely busy over the next few months and I'm going to Vera Cruz tomorrow."

She looks across at him and says:

"Vera Cruz will be a good match for you."

"Vera Cruz is not a woman it's a —"

"I know."

"You know you're crazy? But you make me laugh, and I do, as you put it, desperately want to jump your bones. Can I call you when I get back?"

"Sure, but my cottage may have fallen down by then, so if you call and there's no answer you'll know what happened."

Wedding in Roxbury

ON THE FIRST WARM DAY of the year, my friend Milly says that she knows this chicken place in Roxbury where they have a unique intercom system. She says that it is a square hole in the wall into which you yell your order and somebody inside yells the details of your order back at you. I tell her that she is lying; so she says, "All right, let's leave the city of Cambridge and drive out to Roxbury and see this place for ourselves."

And so we get in her car and go, and sure enough there it is, the Chicken Shack with the natural, organic call-and-response intercom. And we, two grown women, have a good time bawling out:

"A quarter chicken with french fries and coleslaw and a large Pepsi," into a square hole in the side of the building. We also find it uncommonly funny when the voice from within the hole repeats our order and directs us to drive around and pick up our food through a larger hole in the front of the building.

My son Miles is standing up on the backseat. He is seven years old. He asks:

"What's so funny, Auntie Milly?"

It's hard to explain, so we just drive instead, eating greasy chicken and revelling in the sight of the good people of Dorchester and Roxbury wearing their kick-winter-to-the-curb colours. Wicked pepper reds and sun-hot yellows and loud lime greens and ghetto greens outgreening the first leaves that are making a valiant breakthrough after a long, punishing New England winter.

Music is tumbling out of doorways and falling in light showers from upper-storey windows. Is vintage Motown the sound of spring in the Dorchesters and Roxburys of the United States of America? The car is rocking as we drive along to the joyous rhythms of Martha and the Vandellas when we turn a corner and see what looks like at least a hundred people lining the street opposite this big church. A few of them are positioned up on rooftops where they can get a good view; men, women, and children are sitting on stoops, drinking pop, and all are waiting for the commencement of the best entertainment that a poor person can get upon a sunny Saturday afternoon. Milly finds a parking space and we urge a protesting Miles out of the car.

"Why can't we keep driving?"

"Because Aunt Milly and I want to see the wedding."

"But I don't want to see any stupid wedding."

"I'll buy you a pizza after."

"All right then."

The guests are arriving like brightly plumed birds. The guests look like gorgeous tropical birds flying back from the south where they have outwaited winter. Nobody is wearing a dark colour.

Then the first limousine in the bridal party pulls in, carrying the groomsmen. They are suited in powder-blue tuxedoes with broad black cummerbunds. They emerge from the long black limousine and stand fronting and posing on the sidewalk so that we can all get a good look at them.

Says a young girl standing with a group of her friends, who are all wearing brief cut-off shorts:

"The tall, slim one looks good."

"Nah, the other one looks better."

"You mean that heavy-set dude with his belly hanging over his sash."

"He ain't so fat."

"Girl, your taste is in your mouth."

Then another limousine pulls in, long, low, and sleek. This time it's a white one, and out steps the groom and the best man. The groom is wearing a more evolved version of the powder-blue tuxedoes worn by the groomsmen. His is a darker blue, it is silk, and it boasts satin lapels.

"That fat dude you like must be the brother of the groom."

"He sure look just like him."

"I hear he's a Jamaican."

Well at this point I feel really connected to this wedding.

The groom, after all, is my countryman. I bet if my mother were here she would have found out his name and traced his ancestry immediately back to the parish of Hanover.

"Yes, he is a Spence from Patty Hill. Norah Spence was his mother. She was a Campbell before she married Leonard Spence."

And would you know that the minute I finished hearing my mother's voice in my head, somebody in the crowd said:

"His people own a bakery, they make them Jamaican patties."

"From Patty Hill," says my mother's voice.

At this point another limo pulls up and six frilled bridesmaids emerge in frou-frous of mint green, lilac, and blush pink.

Milly decides to approach one of the limousine drivers for more information. The driver looks like an old bop boy. A retired mack daddy. He sports a cascade of shoulder-length, heavily lubricated curls and one cubic zirconia earring. His chauffeur's livery is frayed at the lapels and old-looking, but his hands are weighted with shining rings. It's a wonder this man can lift his hands to the steering wheel. Rings! The only man that I have ever seen wear more rings was Duke Reid the Trojan, the infamous Jamaican record producer whose every finger was be-ringed – people said he was a science man and those rings were guard rings. The limo driver did not seem like a science man, just an old-time player who maybe used to be part-owner of a nightclub but had fallen upon hard times.

The first thing that Milly does is to tell the man that her name is Jeanelle.

"So, Jeanie," says the limo driver, "are you a teacher? You look like a teacher. My second wife was a teacher." Milly/Jeanelle/Jeanie says no, she is a nurse – which is also not true, we are both writers.

The old bop boy then tells her all about the groom's parents. "Yeah, they from Jamaica, come up here and made themselves a fortune off them beef patties and that hard bread."

My people, I am so proud of my people. And the name of the bread is hard-dough bread. Then the biggest, whitest limo of them all pulls up, and a ripple goes through the crowd. "The bride, the bride."

Everybody gathers in closer for a look at the bride.

First the matron of honour rustles onto the pavement in magenta taffeta, and then a short little man who must be the bride's father and a stout lady who must be her mother step out, then finally the bride.

From the very brief glimpse we caught of her, we saw that the bride was as slender as the groom was corpulent, and that she was wearing a long veil over her face and a wide hoop-skirted dress so that she looked like she could be placed on top of the wedding cake, which no doubt would have been baked at the groom's father's bakery.

"She so itty-bitty."

"How she manage a big dude like that?"

We wait outside as the sounds of the wedding ceremony drift out to us in the street and mix with the oldies music coming from the boom boxes on the stoops.

⁓

"My Girl" by the Temptations, that was the song, "the shot" as the groom, a batsman on the West Indies cricket team, might have called it. As a special surprise for his new bride, the star batsman groom had hired a popular singer to serenade them with that song as he and the nice girl exited from Claxton Hall in London after taking their vows, and like every other detail of the wedding, everybody heard about it only after it had all happened.

"The girl should be declared a national heroine."

"That story should be made into a movie."

"Boy, the girl good!"

What had happened was this. There was this really beautiful girl who lived in Jamaica, beautiful not only in that dark-sugar complexion with perfect white teeth way, she was also just a nice person, not bitchy or show off or unkind, just a really nice girl. But she had this boyfriend whom we all called Chief because he must have been a throwback to one of those Old World rulers who was used to having many wives. This guy always had at least three women. The nice girl, another girl who was nowhere as lovely as the nice girl but who was rumoured to be very creative in the boudoir, and a third whom he changed every few months but was usually some very young just-out-of-high-school girl who, as he himself would have said, he was "bringing." Everybody always wondered what the nice girl was doing with a man like that, a man who was not below discussing the shortcomings and virtues of his women in public! "Well, A is really nice, but B is really, really sexy, although A has better legs."

I mean, what kind of a human being is that? Everybody always wondered how the nice girl put up with him. or rather why she put up with him, and why she stayed with him year after year hoping he'd give up B and the ever-changing Cs and settle down with her.

As it turned out, the nice girl loved sports, especially cricket, and once when the West Indies were playing Australia at Sabina Park, she went with a group of her friends, because Chief was the only man in Jamaica who did not like cricket, to cheer on the Windies. They had seats in a box right near the cricket pitch, the equivalent of ringside seats if this were a boxing match, which it was not because it was cricket. The nice girl was wearing a simple orange-coloured dress that showed off her shoulders, which should have been very broad considering all the heavy load she was lifting in the person of Chief, but her shoulders were not so broad, just nicely proportioned to support her slender neck.

According to people who were there, when the Windies filed out of the pavilion on to the field like knights going in to do battle (this was in the days when the West Indies had a cricket team they were really proud of), the crowd went wild and people started singing, "Cricket, lovely cricket, at Lords where I saw it," which didn't really make sense because most of the people who were singing that had never been to Lords, which is in England, but it was really the "Cricket, lovely Cricket" part of the song that was important. As the valiant West Indies team came out onto the field, the nice girl who could also be a fun girl started blowing kisses to them, and the star batsman (who was an upstanding young man from another island) happened to look across and see her, and right away he knew that she was the girl he wanted to give and receive kisses to and from for the rest of his life. A revelation like that could have proved to be a distraction for a lesser man, but not the star batsman. Then and there he decided that he would bat like hell to impress the kiss-throwing nice girl. And boy, did he bat. Boy, did he score, mostly fours and sixes, hardly any singles. He almost broke Sir Garfield Sobers's record of 365 runs not out that day, but rain stopped play right after he hit a six and the ball rose like a round cork bird and winged it over the fence of Sabina Park.

When the match ended, there was a party for the cricketers in the big old Colonial-style club near Sabina Park, and the nice girl and her friends all went along. Legend now has it that the moment she came through the door, the star batsman walked over to her and the first words he ever spoke to her were:

"Is two months long enough to plan our wedding?"

She must have immediately said, "Yes!"

And then one of them must have said something like "But we have to keep it all secret" and either she or the star batsman may have said, "Suits me" as he gathered her into his arms. They danced together for the rest of the night. That is a fact because everybody at the party saw them. The next morning the star batsman left the island along with the rest of the West Indies cricket team.

She never discussed her business with anybody. Nobody. Not even her friends, who took to teasing her about how the star had danced with her all night and who kept asking her if she'd heard from him.

Chief gal-inna-bundle said he'd heard that a "small Island man" had been hitting on her and warned her that he would not tolerate her flirting with other men. She said nothing to him except that she thought that the two of them should take a bit of a break. They'd taken breaks before and they'd always gotten back together, so Chief said a break was all right with him. She said nothing to anybody. She just made her wedding plans and presumably she and the star batsman communicated back and forth over the next two months.

And then she announced that she was going on a visit to London.

And Chief wasn't worried. In fact, he volunteered to drive the nice girl to the airport and marvelled at just why she had so many suitcases but concluded that they were filled with food and Blue Mountain coffee and things from Jamaica that her relatives had requested she bring for them. And the nice girl bid Chief goodbye and boarded a British Airways flight and went to London, where she met the star batsman. Not long after arriving in London, she put on her bridal gown, which she had designed and sewn herself and brought from Jamaica in one of her big suitcases, and she went with the star batsman one morning to Claxton Hall, where they were married. There was a small, tasteful wedding breakfast at the Dorchester Hotel after; then they jetted off to Paris that same afternoon for a sweet honeymoon.

Like everybody else, Chief read about it in the newspapers where he saw the photo of the nice girl now a nice bride, smiling on the arm of the star batsman. For months after Chief kept raging that he could not believe that the nice girl could have been so wicked and deceitful until somebody said to him, "Are you saying that what they did was not cricket?" and that got a big laugh.

The brief report that accompanied the photo said that a popular singer at the time had been hired by the star batsman to serenade him and his bride as they left the church. "My Girl" is what the popular singer sang, and I always remember that story when I hear that song, which has now stopped playing.

Milly and the chauffeur are in deep conversation so I finish my chicken and play with Miles until we hear the organ sound the wedding march. We the people surge forward, we all want to see this tiny little bride and her big and broad Jamaican husband emerge as husband and wife from the church. And when finally they appear through curtains of rice and confetti, we see how she barely makes it to his shoulder even in her very high-heeled shoes, and we see something else very clearly too now that her long veil is lifted.

"Mmm, mmm, the girl pregnant."

"Maybe I could get pregnant by the heavyset brother and have a big wedding too."

"Well, you best get changed out a that raggedy-arse outfit and run over there and catch him before he drive away in that limo."

"Mmm, mmm. Girl about to have that baby any day now."

And I'm thinking, So what? For they both look so happy.

Fat groom from Patty Hill is smiling like he won the lottery. Tiny cute-faced bride is looking peaky, and the front of her dress is riding a little high, but the two of them look like they want to explode with joy, and fatboy groom is handling his little dolly bride with such care, as if he is afraid she will break.

Milly is telling the limo driver that he can call her at Brigham and Women's Hospital, where she does not work. Miles is demanding, "Mother, where is the pizza you promised me?"

And I'm thinking, The best of luck to you both. Good for you, patty youth and dolly bride. May you live happily ever after and laugh in the face of the badmind. Live long and prosper and spread happiness. May yours be the one in however many marriages that lasts till death do you part. Good luck, good luck, and more good luck. I hope that you are still together twenty-five years from now. By then fat groom will be the head of his family's bakery empire and dolly bride will be a plump, middle-aged, very respectable married lady, who will cry shame on young women who get pregnant before they marry.

The Big Shot

ALBERT WOKE UP drenched with sweat, his own heart about to attack him in his chest, the same horrible dream again.

The dream in which he was walking through his old neighbourhood, through West Kingston, past the broken-down houses and the many-roomed government yards, walking past the knots of criminals (everybody there looked like a criminal to him) standing on the street corners, the leaning zinc fences that barely concealed all manner of nameless horrors waiting to jump out and claim him.

"Albert, is you that star?"

"Is when the man come forward?"

"Let off a money, nuh?"

"You see Delzie and the youth yet?"

In the dream the older women always heaped blessings on him and said things like:

"You see him there, me used to change him nappy, you know!"

This dream wouldn't leave him, even after so many years. He was now way past those circumstances and those people, but the dream wouldn't leave him. Even as a child he hated the poverty and looked down on the poor people around him. He was going to get out as soon as he could. He always knew this. He was bright, so much more intelligent than all the other children at his school.

Albert never knew his father. People said he was a university professor for whom Albert's mother used to do domestic work. They said that the professor had fired Albert's mother when she told him she was pregnant and ordered security guards to remove her bodily from the premises when she started waiting for him outside his office to ask him for money. Her mother, Miss Cordy, had taken her in and looked after her and the baby Albert. She'd told her daughter to forget about the professor, to stop making a fool of herself by going up to his office and to just leave him to God.

Two and a half years after Albert was born, his mother got a job in Montego Bay and she left Albert in the care of his grandmother. At first she used to come to see him every few weeks, bringing him toys and bags of soft, brightly coloured sweets she called jujupps. Albert's mother would always end up falling asleep on Miss Cordy's bed whenever she came from Montego Bay to visit, and Miss Cordy would say as she watched her daughter stretched out fully clothed across her bed:

"Beat out. Her body beat out."

Then Cherrilyn's visits became less and less frequent, and on the rare occasions on which she came to see him, the child Albert noticed that his mother always looked exhausted, that she'd taken to wearing a long, straight-haired wig that she'd remove and hang on the bedpost whenever she lay down to sleep on Miss Cordy's bed. He noticed too that she had begun to smell of rum and cigarettes, and sometimes she would look at Albert with tears running down her face and say things like:

"It's through nobody don't know what I go through."

After a while Albert only saw his mother at Christmas and sometimes on his birthday. He overheard his grand-mother telling somebody about his mother working in a "sporthouse."

"Me tell her say, anyhow she try and take the little boy, I call police and make them arrest her."

When Albert turned eleven, he passed his Common Entrance Examinations and the people in the neighbourhood came to congratulate him. "Him is a brains, Miss Cordy, mus be all the fish head you give him . . . God bless him." Miss Cordy accepted the praise: "Ah, my love, the Good Lord help to carry him through, him say him want to go for lawyer nuh."

His mother had sent him a greeting card that said "Congratulations." It had five pounds folded inside it. He had given it to his grandmother, who used it to buy his school uniform. In the one room where Albert lived with his granny, Albert was a prince. Miss Cordy sold fruits and sweets and fritters to the children at the school gate in order for Albert to dress better and eat better than all the other children. Miss Cordy always wore one of two dresses; then she had a white dress for going to church and a pair of good shoes and a hat and precious little else.

Albert and his grandmother slept in the same little room with the board floor that was always shining. The furniture in the room consisted of two single beds, a small table, a straight-backed chair, a rocking chair, and a narrow wardrobe in which Albert and Miss Cordy's clothes were hung.

Miss Cordy's aim in life was for Albert to become a lawyer, and Albert's aim was to move as far away from the poverty and poor people in West Kingston as was possible.

Albert got up out of bed. Prudence, his wife, was fast asleep, "dead to the world" as his grandmother would have said. Sometimes he was amazed at how Miss Cordy spoke through him, although he made a point of never speaking "broken English." Sometimes he could hear himself thinking like her. He went into the kitchen, he particularly liked the kitchen of this house, it was big and cheerful with bright curtains and every imaginable electrical appliance; it looked like a kitchen in *Splendid Homes and Magnificent Gardens*. That is exactly how he wanted it, and that is the look the interior decorator had achieved. He sat in the breakfast nook sipping a cup of brandy and hot milk, trying to soothe himself back to sleep.

Sometimes he thought about the dark, narrow little lean-to they referred to as a kitchen in th`e yard where he had lived with his grandmother. Once or twice when Miss Cordy was sick he had to go into the kitchen to cook . . . the fire wall was black and furry with soot and you had to look for chips of wood all over the yard to help "catch up" the coal fire. Actually, making a fire was something Albert used to get very absorbed in doing. He would fill the bowl of the small cast-iron stove with coals, having raked out the ashes from the previous meal's cooking. Then he'd put the small chips of wood crisscrossing one another in the centre of the bed of coal. Next he'd roll up bits of newspaper that he'd carefully wedge under the arrangement of chips. A little kerosene oil poured over the chips and a match to light it. At first the flame would shoot straight up and you had to be careful if you were bending over the stove. The flame soon died down and then the chips would burn down to conduct fire into the coals. You had to keep fanning the fire awhile with a piece of cardboard or an old almanac or even a piece of tin, like the lid of a kerosene tin that was used to boil white clothes.

Albert was a very methodical person and he remembered every detail of lighting fires in the tenement yard kitchen. So when he inclined the knob of his big shining gas stove and the clean blue flame rose up as high or as low as he wanted it to go, his heart would rise too, for he had made it. The dream usually flew the gate for bad memories. Hard on the heels of catching up the fire was of course remembering Delzie and the baby, the teenaged child it would now be; the child she said was his.

Miss Cordy had called Albert into the room. He had been sitting outside on a bench trying to read a book by the light of a bottle torch. He could have gone inside the room and read by the light of the bare fifteen-watt bulb that hung on a wire from the ceiling, but sometimes he could not abide the physical closeness with his grandmother, her old-lady smell and her complaints about her various aches and pains; he was also wanting to avoid her because he was in trouble.

"Yes, Granny?"

"Albert, is true say Delzie pregnant and she call your name?"

He stood before his grandmother with his head held down, his face burning with shame.

"Yes, ma'am."

"Well, since you done pass out your exam and we done decide say you going to England already, just as cheap you go right now. Me never bring you so far fi throwaway yourself pon a little black girl like Delzie." And the move was decided as simply as that. Albert and his granny kept a conspiracy of silence. Nobody in the yard or the neighbourhood knew when he left for England. No cars filled with well-wishers had gone to the airport to see him off. No friends and relatives stood on the waving gallery to wave at him until he disappeared inside the plane. He left without saying a word to Delzie, whose pregnancy had not yet begun to show, so he never did see her with her "belly." Back in those days he used to wonder who the child would look like, would it be a boy or girl? Then he stopped wondering and came to the conclusion that none of that had any bearing on him or his life.

About six months after he reached London and was beginning to be settled in the English life, he received a letter from his mother.

Dear Son,

I regret to tell you that your grandmother take sick and she passed away. I had was to come to town and bury her. All her thoughts was of you. Please don't

forget to remember me, study hard, and make yourself
into real big shot.

Your loving mother,
Cherrilyn Brown

Albert stayed in his room for days crying for Miss Cordy,
who was the only person he had ever really loved, who loved
him more than herself. As for his mother, he never wrote to
her again after he sent her £5 toward "expenses."

After Albert had run off to England without telling her, leaving
her behind with her belly, Delzie's young life had gone
to hell. Her parents, who were churchgoing people, were so
ashamed that she had disgraced their family name that they
had sent her away to stay with one of her aunts in her spacious
house in Bournemouth Gardens in East Kingston. Her
aunt, as it turns out, was glad to take in the fallen girl because
it meant she did not have to pay a maid to help her with all
the domestic work that was required to keep her lovely house
spotless. Delzie's water broke while she was kneeling down
to scrub the cold tile floors of a bathroom.

Delzie gave birth to Albert's son down at Victoria Jubilee
Hospital, known as Lineen. She shared a bed with another
teenaged mother who kept screaming terrible bad words.
Delzie had listened to the other girl and had sworn she would
not behave like that. When her labour pains intensified she
just loudly begged God to take her. When the child was born,
her relatives asked her what his name was and she said,
"Albert Stephenson." They had been so angry. "Have sense.

You don't see Albert gone leave you, him don't want neither you nor the child, so why you going to go and give it him name?" Delzie had remained silent and she had registered the child in the name of Albert Stephenson.

Before Delzie met Lynval, she used to think there was no justice in the world. Lynval was her husband, the father of her two daughters and her baby son.

Lynval had made her know just how caring a relationship between a man and a woman could be. When she had become pregnant, for him a beautiful and tender scenario began to unfold between them. Lynval bringing her some special little sweet something to eat every evening. Lynval rubbing her big belly with cocoa butter. Lynval hurrying home to cook the dinner for the first month because the smell of cooking oil nauseated her, and she calling him "Papa" and referring to him as "The Baby Father" and she staying up late every night the week before she went to hospital to have the baby, washing and ironing all his clothes so that he could go to work clean and tidy while she was in the hospital. When she took in, in the middle of the night, Lynval went to wake up the taximan who lived three streets away and held her in his arms all the way to Lineen.

Albert became used to the English way of life very easily. It was as if all the time he had been in rehearsal for a move up to a higher quality lifestyle. Anybody who ever saw him in a pub drinking a pint of bitter and ordering a ploughman's lunch would swear that Albert was an Englishman. He developed a taste for the warm, amber-coloured lager that was pulled in the London pubs; and he was fond of telling his new English friends the story about how some foreign chemists had visited Jamaica and had been asked to run some blind tests on the beers brewed on the island:

"When the tests came back, they recommended that the horses should be shot!"

That story always got a laugh.

He studied hard and did well at his exams and went out with a number of English girls who found him very attractive. The one woman he would like to have married was Joan. Big, blonde, pretty Joan who came from a titled British family. She was always laughing and she believed that life should not be taken seriously. One weekend while her parents were away on a holiday in Corfu, she had taken Albert with her up to their family home in the Lake District. He'd arranged to meet her outside the Inns of Court because he did not want her to see the run-down rooming house owned by a Jamaican couple he lived in off Bayswater Road. He'd also had no idea how to dress for a weekend in the country, so he wore one of the two black suits and white shirts that he wore every day and in a small suitcase, or "grip" as his grandmother would have called it, he carried a change of underwear and a sweater.

"We'll have to get you some proper clothes," Joan said when she rolled up in a dark-green Range Rover. She wore a cream silk scarf printed with black and brown horses tied over her hair and knotted under her chin, and she had on yellow suede driving gloves. She took him over to Marks and Spencers on Oxford Street and made him try on a pair of brown corduroy trousers, a tan-coloured sweater, and a red flannel shirt. When Albert tried to explain with some embarrassment that he did not have the money to pay for these clothes, she brushed him off with:

"My treat, love."

He had never accepted anything like clothes from a woman before. He'd never sat in a car driven by a woman before. All the way up to the Lake District he marvelled at how expertly Joan handled the big square vehicle, pointing out various places along the way, skilfully changing lanes, making her way up the M6 with the greatest of ease.

When they reached just outside Grasmere, Albert asked Joan to stop and allow him to open the door and climb down from the car that rode so high up on the road. He felt an urge to walk way out into one of the wide green fields and to fall down on his knees by the banks of the shining Derwent waters.

If he lived in a place like this he could pretend that he was "born big so," as his grandmother would have said. He could forget about his grandmother and his mother and Delzie and all the other benighted poor stupid people he'd grown up with. If he lived in a place like this he could forget about them all. The thought came to him that if he could marry laughing, carefree Joan they could live up in the Lake District. They could raise horses, even though he didn't know a thing about horses; surely he could learn.

That night over supper she prepared in the big draughty kitchen of her parents' two-hundred-and-fifty-year-old house, Albert suggested marriage to her. Joan put down the bone-handled carving knife that she'd been using to slice away at the boiled gammon to be served with new potatoes and peas and said:

"Oh love, my parents would just die of mortification. Why don't we just have fun?"

And they did, right there in every room of the two-hundred-and-fifty-year-old house, including in her parents' bedroom, where a huntsman in a red jacket, mounted on a white horse, rode furiously across the dusty tapestry that hung behind the massive oak bed.

But much as he enjoyed the British way of life, Albert knew that the chances of him making it really big in his field were slim. He was not a fool; when he looked in the mirror he saw himself. He was a slim, very elegant, light-brown man, and, although his nose was straight enough and his lips were not too thick and his hair was cut low enough to look not so kinky, he was not an Englishman.

He eventually married Prudence, a nurse whose parents were Jamaican but she had been born in England. From the beginning of the marriage she took over the running of their finances; and eighteen months after they married they moved back to Jamaica, where Albert joined a well-established firm of criminal lawyers and Prudence found a job at a private hospital where she was not averse to working round the clock. Their joint incomes enabled them to buy a fine house in Cherry Blossom Gardens within a year of their coming home.

Albert never once visited the old neighbourhood, and whenever he met somebody he used to know from his childhood he'd become very formal and very businesslike.

"Yes, I'm Albert Stephenson, what's your name again? Right. Well, it was good to see you."

And he moved briskly off before they could beg for money or a favour.

After three years of trying without success to conceive, Prudence suggested to Albert that they could adopt a Jamaican child. Albert had not even bothered to answer her when she'd said that, he'd just given her a hard, angry look because he knew that their inability to have children was clearly her fault, not his.

Albert moved easily into the tennis-playing, smart, middle-class, Benz-driving set and his taste for fine clothes made him look like what Miss Cordy and his mother wanted him to be: a qualified big shot. Life was going mostly great except for the dream.

Albert went back to bed soothed by the brandy and dreamt he was made a High Court Judge.

Then one scorching hot afternoon after appearing in court on behalf of a man who'd embezzled millions of dollars from an insurance company, Albert got into his car and started the drive downtown to his office only to find that the air-conditioning system had broken down. He was so hot and miserable that by the time he'd fought his way through the afternoon traffic he'd taken off the jacket and tie that he always wore under his silk robes and rolled up his shirt sleeves.

His secretary remarked, when he got to the office, that she's never seen him without his jacket and tie before, and he said something about him still not being used to the heat and asked her to bring him a cold beer from the refrigerator. She brought the beer to him in his office and as he sipped it he looked through the papers on his desk. Near the bottom of the pile he found a message that a Mrs. Hyacinth Goodman had come to the office to speak to him. He did not recognize the name.

He had just tilted the bottle to his head to down the last of the cold Red Stripe beer when the secretary called in to say Mrs. Goodman had returned and could he see her. He told the secretary to send her in.

In walked Delzie.

Standing in his office was Delzie: older, fatter, with her side teeth missing, but unmistakably Delzie. Her face had not changed much, she was still attractive in an honest, simple kind of way. Albert immediately felt the need to urinate.

She looked right into his face when she spoke to him.

"Albert, you remember me?"

"And what can I do for you?"

"You really going to sit down there like you don't remember me?"

"What is your reason for coming here?"

Delzie had not set out to aggravate Albert, but since he seemed bent on behaving as if he'd never seen her before in his life she heard herself say:

"Albert, you don't remember me from No. 12 Septimus Street, where you grow with your granny Miss Cordy with her two frock? Miss Cordy who used to sell fruits out at the school gate after your mother – who dead some years now in a sporthouse in Montego Bay – go away and leave you?"

Albert gripped the beer bottle hard when he heard mention of his mother whom he had made no move to contact since he'd come back to Jamaica. Some part of him felt relieved to hear that she was dead, and that there was no chance of her turning up at his office like Delzie. He'd imagined that this scenario might occur one day, but he always imagined that she would have announced herself as Delzie whatever the hell her last name was, and that he would have told the secretary to tell her that he was not in. He felt a great pressure building in his bladder.

"Look, I have a client coming in five minutes, I need you to state your business quickly or I'm afraid I'm going to have to ask you to leave."

Delzie stood there looking at Albert, remembering how he and she used to joke with each other innocently, until the night his grandmother had gone to church and he invited her into the room he shared with Miss Cordy, so that he could "show her something."

She remembers how she had liked him so much, she had willingly gone with him that night and several other nights after that when she was only sixteen years old and so very trusting.

The sight of Albert sitting behind a massive mahogany desk in an office that was way bigger than the room he grew up in, the Albert who refused to address her by her name, who so far has shown no indication that he knows who she is, suddenly made Delzie feel very small, so small, she thought to herself that maybe she should just turn around and leave.

God knows she had suffered enough shame and embarrassment because of him, but her reason for coming to see Albert trumped all her embarrassment; she found her voice and said:

"Me personally don't want anything from you, Albert."

"So what the hell are you doing here then?"

"Your son."

"My son? My wife and I have no children. I have no son. I suggest you find one of those other men you were mixing up with to saddle with your problems."

"Yes, your son. If you kill me dead, is your son. You could cut off mi neck, is your son. Him is the dead stamp of you, and you is the first man and the only man I did know."

"Would you lower your voice, this is an office."

"Oh you feel I can't see that for myself? You know something, you really is a facety son of a bitch, you know, you could climb high little more, but you really still sneaking and low."

"Are you insane? Do you want me to call the security guard to put you out on the street where you belong?"

"If me insane, is you mad me. Albert, I never come here today with the intention of having no fuss with you, me forget bout you long time. But you son, yes you son, get involve and police hold him. I only come here today to see if since you turn big lawyer you could do something to help him. But you know something, I don't want anything from you, you see yourself, you look like a idiot. You hear yourself, 'this his han hoffice.' Gwey. Albert, you confuse. You don't know who you is, try find you real self, then maybe you can help somebody. Right now you need help more than me."

"Delzie, go back to Jones Town, that is where rubbish like you belong, take you rass outta my fucking office."

Reaching for the empty beer bottle, he breaks it on the edge of his desk, feeling a hot wet rush down his leg as he jumps to his feet, screaming:

"You want to come draw me back down into your dirty, depraved ghetto life!"

He curses so loudly that everyone, including his secretary and the other lawyers and their clients, came crowding into his office to find out what was causing him to behave in this appalling way.

Delzie was smiling to herself as she hurried out of Albert's office. The fact that she and what she represented had been able to trigger off such a violent response in him was somehow strangely satisfying. To see him reduce himself like that before all his other big-shot colleagues could never make up for what she had suffered because of him, but it did at least give the lie to his pretending that he did not know her, that she was nobody, that she had never been a part of his life.

Her husband, Lynval, was a much better man than Albert any day. Lynval had never treated her son, Albert, differently from their other children, but the boy had something of his father in him. Like, he was always in a hurry, always wanting what their poor but honest existence couldn't provide. The police had held him, saying he was involved in housebreaking and larceny. Lynval was out looking bail for him. She never told him of her plan to go to Albert, his father, for help. She decided she would not tell him where she had been. She and Lynval would just have to go on struggling with their eldest child.

After Delzie left the office that day, the senior partners in the law firm drafted a letter to Albert informing him that they would have to let him go if he ever created that kind of disturbance in their chambers again. Every day Albert worries that Delzie will come back to his office. At night his old dreams continue with a new dimension. In them he becomes a judge and a young man who looks exactly like him is brought up before him for committing unspeakable crimes.

Pinky's Fall

$\sim$

IF ANYTHING, Miss Chin looked more like an Indian. She might have had some distant Chinese relatives somewhere in her bloodlines, but she claimed even stronger Chinese ancestry than her husband, Mr. Chin, who could speak almost no English and had not too long come from Hong Kong.

Miss Chin used to sit in the grocery shop that she operated with Mr. Chin, and she would a talk a lot. At least it seemed that way to me. Every time my mother would send me to buy a tin of condensed milk or a thick, white, hard-dough bread for supper, she would be sitting in the shop talking loudly to whoever happened to be there. Invariably she was holding forth upon the same topic, the dirty, nasty ways of other people's children. And as always, in the same way you said "amen" at the end of a prayer or "goodbye" when you were leaving a place, she would seal her dissertation with a short or long hymn on the virtues of her daughter, Pinky.

Now depending on who was listening (and some poor person was always listening), she could go on for a very long time upon this subject. If the person listening was trying to credit some groceries, she made them listen for a very long time and they, naturally wanting to get the food, would agree with her, the intensity of their agreement depending on the urgency of their need for the food.

Some people, though, like my mother, she never tried that with. My mother did not believe in trusting food. She had a proper shop book and she took her groceries each week and paid promptly for them at the end of the next week. Also my mother had a lot of children and since Miss Chin's problem centred around the dreadful, disgusting, awful behaviour of other people's children, she tended to leave our family alone . . . besides, we were not ordinary, as my mother never ceased to tell us, and, somehow, most people seemed to believe that.

"People who don't love children can be hard. If you ever hear what Miss Chin said about those two little girls that Mrs. Chambers have."

Miss Chin had one child, her daughter, Pinky, who was not really her daughter, at least that is what other people said. They said Pinky was really the daughter of Miss Chin's sister who was bad and had given birth to Pinky while she was still a schoolgirl.

We never knew what the real story was, but in the Chinese tradition, she held up Pinky as a symbol of purity and goodness. You see Pinky there (concluding passage in today's sermon on the sins of Miss Iris's daughter Cherry, who was spotted by Miss Chin laughing uproariously at the antics of drunken Valbert as he danced the yank to the latest Fats Domino song outside Mr. Albert's bar).

"Pinky never even look through the window when she hear all them kind of things going on, you know. All them kind of rag song don't interest her. When she come home from school, she just go upstairs and you don't hear a sound from her. Sometimes I have to call her and say, 'Pinky, come down and rest your eyes, I don't want to have to buy glasses for you while you so young.' I tell you, we know how to raise children properly, man."

The truster nods . . . and says something like, "Well fancy that, eh . . . the little girl have ambition." Miss Chin did not like me. She said: "Puss bruk coconut in that little girl eye." That was the most she ever said about me that I heard. I heard this because my friend Bev heard her telling this to Bev's Aunt Dolly, and naturally Bev told me. I told my mother, who was furious. She said, "You know I never think badly of other people's children," and she pumped furiously at her sewing machine.

One day I heard the girls in the sewing room talking. Edith, my favourite of all the girls my mother taught to sew, said to Janette, a girl who always wore her man's hat (she did this to show his other girlfriends that she was the one he lived with): "Guess who fall?" Janette, running the pinking shears down the seam of a dress and leaving a row of pointed teeth along the seam, said, "Who?" Edith said, "Pinky." Janette dropped the garment she was finishing and screamed, "You lie!"

Pinky the perfect was quite pregnant. She had suddenly disappeared from the rooms above the shop and, according to Miss Olga, the lady who worked for Miss Chin and

Mr. Chin, it was not even Miss Chin who had found out. It seemed Pinky had confessed her terrible secret to Mr. Chin. The women of the area were appalled that Miss Chin did not, as they all did, check upon their daughter's monthly health. For it seemed that Pinky was almost four months' pregnant by the time the whole story came to light.

Four months' pregnant by, of all people, Black Boy, the young man who swept out the shop and did all the dirty work, like chopping up the saltfish and the corn pork. In a way it was not difficult to understand. It must have been unbearably lonely for her up there in her castle above the shop with no one good enough to be her friend . . . Pinky fall. I can just imagine what my mother was going to say when she heard this.

The Dolly Funeral

~

I CAN'T REMEMBER how Bev and I became friends, but I remember at first feeling displaced by her as leader of our neighbourhood group of children at large, in the summer holidays. She came from a family that was even bigger than mine and up until that time I had been the child to hold that particular distinction. I had six brothers, which meant people thought twice about interfering with me. Bev had eight brothers. My parents had nine children. There were twelve children in the Lyons' household, and when her family moved into the neighbourhood, she just naturally assumed the leadership role that I had held till then. I loved visiting the Lyons' house. They lived in "their own place," which made them rich in the eyes of everyone in the neighbourhood. Their place was a many-roomed yard peopled by the many Lyons' married sons and daughters and a few aunts, uncles, and cousins.

The first time I visited their house, I remember wishing that I lived there. Unlike my house, where somebody was always correcting you for "sitting down bad" or "common behaviour," the Lyons were a marvellously free and uninhibited people.

They yelled at each other, screamed with laughter, and used language that would send my mother for the brown soap to scour out somebody's mouth.

The first time I witnessed Mrs. Lyons trying to discipline Vavan, "the baby" of the family, I was truly astonished. Vavan did some really dreadful thing, Mrs. Lyons screamed at him to "beyave," he replied, "Gweyframme." She swung a punch at him, he stuck out his tongue at her, dropped to his belly, wriggled under the bed, and from his dark hideout proceeded to tell her some things no child should tell a mother and remain alive. She yelled that she was going to tear his backside and, seizing a broom, commenced to stab wildly at his hidden form. She must have seen me staring at her because she paused and advised me to go outside and play in the yard, then they resumed the duel, he with the foul mouth and she with the broomstick.

All sorts of wonderful things happened at the Lyons' house. Periodic fights would break out between the brothers: big, strong Spanish-looking men who would fight each other fiercely until their mother appeared and sometimes doused them with a goblet of cold water.

My friend Bev had all sorts of lovely toys and games to play with, but mostly she had a wonderful talent for organizing great events. These could range from the really low-level act of getting a group of children together to go and tease Rose — the retarded child who lived several streets away (I can truly say I could never bring myself to join in this activity), to informing on Mr. Frenchie to her aunt Miss Dottie about which bar he had spent all his money in (she always told her to mind her own business and stay out of big people's business), to organizing dolls' tea parties, weddings, and pregnancies, to the Dolly Funeral.

One day, toward the end of the summer holidays when it seemed we had run out of new games to play and that Bev's reputation for inspiring leadership of our group was beginning to pall, Bev came up with the idea of the Dolly Funeral. She proceeded to kill one of her less attractive dolls, by wringing its rubber neck, and placed it in a shoe box on her bed. "She dead," said Bev in a low voice. "We going to have to bury her." For two days the doll lay in the "dead house," as Bev referred to the shoe box, her life all bubbled out in clouds of pink and white foam, while we prepared for the funeral.

We searched my mother's sewing scraps for some white satin and lace material and we sewed her a lovely shroud. Bev's brother Harry proceeded to nail up a crude coffin using what looked like boards ripped from the side of the pit latrine; all arrangements for the funeral were organized by Bev.

First there would be a procession from the front gate through the middle gate (her yard had two separate sections) and down to the graveside, which was situated under a huge ackee tree. I was not so thrilled to hear about the choice of this site as large rats were known to live in the ackee tree and I was more afraid of them than most other things, but I had to go along with Bev's plans.

We all went to inspect the gravesite, which had been dug by Harry, Bev's brother, with one of Mrs. Lyons' cooking spoons. There were to be some light refreshments as it was necessary to attract as many children as possible to this event. The refreshments consisted of pieces of bulla cake and lime-less limeade known as belly-wash.

The funeral arrangements fully occupied us for two days. Bev was going to be the parson. When the boys remarked that nobody had ever seen a woman parson, she just looked at them and said, "Is whose dolly funeral?" and they retreated. I was going to read from the Bible because I could read better than any of the other children, or so they said anyway.

My mother was not consistent when it came to allowing me to play at other people's houses. Some days for no reason, she would say, "Don't leave the house today. Sometimes you should let people long to see you." The day of the funeral was one of those days. I got dressed to walk over to Bev's house and as I approached my mother to ask her permission/inform her where I was going, she said, "Don't leave the house, etc."

I pleaded with her, I inquired of her if she did not remember me telling her all about the arrangements for the funeral, how important it was that I go because I was going to read from the Bible and could she "just please do, I beg you, Mama, make me go." My mother started the sewing machine by slapping the rim of the handle with her palm and proceeded to pump the broad flat pedal at a fierce rate. That action, read by any fool, clearly meant, "Don't say anymore."

So I subsided in a corner of the veranda and wept. As with each time I felt I had been dealt an injustice by my parents, I imagined that I was not their child. That I had been the victim of a careless hospital blunder and that my real parents were out there somewhere in Kingston. Nice people, who would never deprive me of the right to attend a Dolly Funeral.

As the time of the funeral approached, Bev came over to inquire why I was not present at the site and saw me sobbing on the veranda. I told her what my mother had said; she said, kissing her teeth, "Chuh just teef out," and I for the first time in my life did just that, I sneaked out of the yard without my mother's permission. But I had to do it in stages. When Bev had left, I got up from my corner (after a suitable period of time) and made my move, first to the cistern where I drank some water I did not want, then from the cistern when Miss Minnie our helper's back was turned, to the back gate where I stood for some time looking forlornly over the zinc fences and across the gully.

After stage three came the quick, bold dash to freedom. As I took to my heels and headed for Bev's house looking in no other direction but straight ahead, was it paranoia or did I really hear Miss Minnie calling, "Don't your mother tell you not to leave the yard?"

I arrived at a very key moment in the funeral proceedings. It was near the beginning and it was nearly the ending as Vavan chopped Hugh Lawrence Brown (for some reason everybody called this boy all of his entire name all the time) with the same cooking spoon used to dig the grave, in a dispute over who was to carry the coffin. It was a tiny wound really and we persuaded Hugh Lawrence Brown not to go and tell his mother. We had to bribe him by breaking the rules and giving him a whole bulla cake for himself. He ate it right there at the start of the funeral and Harry proceeded to make a bitter remark about "hungry-belly children who just come to nyam off people food." Apart from these set-backs, the procession went as planned. We lowered the doll into the grave and heaped up a mound of dirt into the hole. We then stuck a cross made from two fudgesticks wired together with an elastic band at the head of the grave.

We attempted to sing "Abide with Me," but nobody knew all the words, so we sang instead "Flow Gently, Sweet Afton," which we had all learned at school. I read Psalm 1 rather badly and too loudly because I was afraid of the rats and of the wrath of my mother, who must have found out that I was missing by now.

Even as I read, I imagined myself beneath the ground in a simple wooden box because my mother was surely going to kill me when I went home. She didn't. My father almost did. He whom I loved so much because he was never cross with me. It was the worst beating I ever received, not that he beat me badly, but to be beaten by somebody you loved so much was so humiliating. He said he had to because I had been "wilfully disobedient." He forbade me to visit Bev's house for at least two weeks, and by the end of the two weeks school had started again and Bev got herself a boyfriend and told me I was a child and she couldn't play with me anymore. But I never did hear of anybody else having a Dolly Funeral, and even though I got punished for going, I'm glad I went. No matter what. So there.

Fool-Fool Rose Is Leaving
Labour-in-Vain Savannah

WHEN HUGH LAWRENCE BROWN, Vavan, Tiny — whose father went by the unusual name of Merrimen — and Mary and Joseph, the brother and sister who lived off the charity of the nuns and priests at St. Anne's Church, and Dreamy and Winston were all assembled, Bev told Hugh Lawrence Brown that he was the one who had been appointed to go to Rose's gate and ask her mother to allow her to come out and play.

"Why me? When Rose mother find out say is tease we come tease Rose, is me she going hate."

"Hugh Lawrence Brown," said Bev, "you are a real girl child."

Well, that almost started a fight right there, so the expedition to go and tease Rose was nearly aborted, but Bev was a strong leader, she half-apologized to Hugh Lawrence Brown: "Cho, Hugh Lawrence Brown, you can't take a little joke?"

And the mission was brought back on track. "You coming?" she then says to me.

"No."

"Why?"

"Because I don't see what kind of fun you get out of teasing Rose."

"Because she fool-fool just like you."

"And you are a dutty dog."

When I said that, Bev shoved me, and all the children started yelling, "Fight! Fight!" and Vavan picked up some pebbles and jiggling them in his palm, chanted, "Hot patty! Hot patty!"

Bev boxed the pebbles out of his hand to show that she accepted the challenge to fight and then she turned and beat me up.

Even as a child of nine as I was then, I could not fight. I could always read well and write good compositions, that is why I became a teacher, but to this day I still cannot fight. So Bev thumped me up good and proper and then departed, surrounded by her cheering fans, chanting:

"Fool-fool Rose, fool-fool Rose, lift up your frock and take off your clothes!" Rose would strip herself naked when she heard that.

My mother, like every mother in the neighbourhood, believed that Bev, whose full name was Bevonia, was too womanish and out of order. If I went home and told my mother that Bev had just beaten me up she would say, "It serves you right, you should keep better company."

The shadows under her eyes were dark as bruises. My nephew's wife could hardly wait to pull her into the house, and without telling her good morning or asking her how she was feeling she says:

"Lord, you look terrible, m'dear, you look like hell."

And I think to myself, "That's right, dear, build her right up, give her a boost."

She did not offer her a cup of coffee or tea, although it was early in the morning. Every day I find myself wondering who raised this young woman that my nephew just married.

For twenty-seven years I have lived in this house helping my late sister, who was a famous person, to raise her family. Please don't ask me what I have to show for all those years. I came here after I was disappointed in love and my sister suggested then that I should come and spend time with her and her family and help her to look after her children till I recovered. I came and I stayed. I once saw a program on television about lions. It said that sometimes in a pride there is an aunt lion who never mates, she just stays and helps her sister lion to raise the cubs. My sister passed a year ago and willed the family home to her youngest son. Before she died, she suggested that I build a prefabricated two-room flat in the backyard. My youngest nephew has recently revived this plan to give me shelter in a prefabricated house in what is now his backyard. I heard his wife say to her friend that one day in the future they will rent it to a university student.

My nephew's wife now pulls the girl inside and starts to interrogate her.

"So what? He beat you? Yes, he beat you up, look at your face!"

The girl shakes her head and whispers,

"No, he didn't touch me."

You can see that she is deeply disappointed to hear this because she was already rehearsing the telephone calls she would make to her other friends the minute that this poor weeping one left. My nephew's wife is truly disappointed, but I have a feeling that she will make something of the beating story anyway.

"M'dear had to call you. The damn idiot just left here, you want to see how it look bad. It need to go to the hairdresser and it have on a cheap-looking old woman frock. It claim that it loser husband never beat her, but her eyes look well bruised to me. I think that she's too ashamed to admit that he buss her arse."

Not so; for some of the things that I have heard that girl come here and reveal about herself to that young woman in there whom she calls her friend should only be confessed to a priest.

"Fool-fool Rose, lift up your dress and take off your clothes." And poor Rose with her slant eyes and her broad flat face, and her nose always running, lifts up her dress and strips herself naked before Bev and company.

Sometimes when I hear that young miss in there emptying her guts before my nephew's dear wife, I want to run in there and clamp my hand over her mouth.

"I asked him for house money last night, he got into one disgraceful temper and went on so bad that all the neighbours could hear, telling me how I was nothing but a effing parasite."

"I said I wasn't going to tell you this, but this friend of mine who flies for Bee Wee, she used to go with your husband. As a matter of fact she tell me that up to last month he was still trying to check her, she said that he used to slap her up. You sure he doesn't beat you?"

"No, when he gets drunk he just curse me like a dog."

"Just curse?"

"Yes."

When she does not catch any scandal fish with her beating bait, my nephew's wife asks her friend right out: "So, is he still . . . you know . . . sleeping with you?"

I figured that this would be a good time to go into the living room and to offer the poor young woman a cup of tea. I went in, handed her the cup, and looked straight into her eyes.

"Here, young miss, drink this and you will feel better."

"So where is my tea, Aunt Ivy?"

"But didn't my nephew bring you breakfast in bed this morning?"

She gives a brittle little laugh like one of those women on the soap operas she likes to watch when I say this. She flicks off imaginary crumbs from her purple and gold dressing gown with her right hand where her topaz dinner ring gleams like one eye of a brindle puss. All this is to show this poor unfortunate one what a fabulous life she is living. She bought that ring from a friend of hers who drives around in a big Mercedes-Benz and sells jewellery. I call that higglering. I don't think that she and her friends would call it that.

All of this is taking place on the white sofa in the all-white living room. When they got married, my nephew and his wife modernized the family home; everything in this house is now mostly white, white with chrome accents. They even sprayed my mother's mahogany dining table and chairs, which my sister laid claim to before my mother had barely closed her eyes, white! This means everyone has to leave their shoes at the front door at all times and there is a helluva of commotion if so much as a spot gets on the white carpet. When I saw that they had furnished the house in white, I said to my nephew: "So what is going to happen when you have children?"

"We don't want any."

Well, that's that.

Anyway, my nephew's wife's friend did not stay long today. My nephew's wife gave her short shrift because she is throwing a dinner party tonight to which said friend is not invited and she needs to spend time rearranging the furniture. The food is going to be catered. I'm just asked to bake my famous soft-top potato pudding, which I have baked every single Saturday that I have been in this house. My secret is to add a judicious pinch of black pepper to the batter.

You know my friend Edith never stopped writing to me from Canada from the time I moved into this house asking me if I did not want a life for myself. I always replied to her that my being with my sister's children was just like having my own. Edith once cut out an article from the *Calgary Herald* headlined: "DON'T PITY THIS SINGLE WOMAN." I remember what a chuckle I got from it when the writer said that she was the woman with the broadest of smiles on her face as she strode happily through the shopping mall, spending her money as she pleased with no one to answer to. Edith wrote in the margin: *I know how she feels, you could feel like her too.*

I have many regrets. One of my biggest ones is that I did not get out my papers when I had the chance, to go and live with my friend Edith in Calgary when she kept suggesting it years ago. I said I could not leave because I was really needed here in this house. Poor Edith went and got Alzheimer's and started writing me letters telling me about somebody's "Rawrse" and their "bamboo cloth." I guess she never cursed those words when she was herself so she could not spell them either. Anyway she is now languishing in a nursing home and that is the end of me and the going to live in Calgary, Alberta, story.

"If you ever hear what Rose say to me this morning," I remember Rose's mother saying, she talked about Rose as if she were just like all the other children even though the other mothers jeered at her behind her back and said that Rose was just like a dumb animal.

"Rose say: 'Mama, Wose want go school.'"

So her mother sent her to school and one of the teachers at All Saints School said that trying to teach Rose was like cultivating at Labour-in-Vain Savannah, a place in the parish of St. Elizabeth where no matter how hard the farmers tried, nothing they planted would ever grow because the ground was tough, unyielding, and barren.

My mother was very upset when she heard that and said: "Everybody can be taught something."

But as God would have it, Rose's mother went to work as a domestic helper with an Englishwoman who trained dogs, and because Rose was "unteachable" or "ineducable" she began to take Rose to work with her. The woman, whose name was Miss Priestman, took a liking to Rose and taught her to read by repeating things over and over and over and over again, just like she did when she was training the dogs. And as it turns out, something about Rose – whether it was her thick body smell or the droning, humming sound she always made to herself like bees in a logwood thicket – had a special effect on the dogs. It's as if they relaxed completely when Rose was around and so she was able to help the English lady to give medicine to the sickest, crossest dogs.

When the nuns at St. Anne's heard about this, they presented Rose with a broach with an image of St. Francis of Assisi on it, and Sister Philomena told everybody that Rose was specially blessed by that beloved patron saint of animals. After that everybody started making much of Rose and bringing their dogs and cats for her to bless.

"Rose, you can just bless Fluffy for me? The other day a Huntington's Bakery bread cart lick him and look how him walk and limp now."

Rose became much in demand as a blesser of animals, and that is when she stopped playing with Bev and stopped lifting up her dress and stripping herself naked.

My nephew's wife often she rises up early and goes out to shop for more things for the white house. This morning soon after she drives out, her friend drives in asking for her. Her face is pale as a calico sheet, so I tell her to come in and sit down in the kitchen while I make her a cup of tea. This lovely-looking young woman, who must be somebody's good good daughter, just sits down there staring out through the big plate-glass window in the white kitchen. She has lost herself outside there somewhere between the big, webbed, satellite dishes and the huge red-ink clouds of bank overdrafts that hover over upper St. Andrew and the last thing that this poor young woman needs is to expose herself anymore to the mistress of the white house.

And so I decide to tell her about fool-fool Rose.

I conclude the story by saying, "So I always said that if even fool-fool Rose could benefit from dog instructions and stop exposing herself to Bev and her gang who only had her as a poppy-show, then I am sure that anybody can do the same." Just then I looked out the window and saw my nephew's wife's car at the top of the avenue.

The young woman sat down there stirring and stirring the tea, making no move to lift the thin white cup to her lips. Then just before my nephew's wife enters the kitchen, she takes a long swallow, picks up her car keys, and gets to her feet as the mistress of the white house comes in saying, "Oh my God, you look like death, and don't even bother to try and tell me this morning that he didn't beat you."

But she tells my nephew's wife that she cannot stay to talk because she waited so long for her that she is now late for a doctor's appointment. I don't know if she is telling the truth or not, but as I watch her get into her car and drive off, I know that it is too late for me to leave, but I do hope and pray that this time fool-fool Rose is really leaving Labour-in-Vain Savannah.

Angelita and Golden Days

ANGELITA BEGAN to notice that every time Golden Days passed through the market, something happen. Hear him coming now singing "Golden Days." Like Mario Lanza, "Golden Days" he was singing and Golden Days they call him because his skin was such an unusual golden colour. When the sun shone on him he seemed to glow and his hair was kind of rusty-looking and he was always dressed in something gold. Like today he was wearing a gold-coloured shirt with a big gold star on one pocket and he was singing rich and golden, like Mario Lanza. Sometimes he did not pass through the market for weeks, then one Saturday morning (you would hear him before you saw him) his notes would float above the heads of the Saturday morning market crowd, rising high above the calls of:

"Yam and potato, ah me have it."

"Buy something from me, nuh nice lady."

"Camphor balls and seasoning, pattanize me nuh, darling."

And the wailing keening of the sankeys sung by the revivalists and the dub dance-hall tapes barking from scattered tape decks and the bad words and the laughter and the greetings and scandal that was the soundtrack accompanying Saturday morning in the market. Miraculously, Golden Days's voice could rise above all that. Hear him now coming, singing "Golden Days" until finally he reaches up to where Angelita is sitting selling her callaloo and pak choi. Half-Indian Angelita with her dress lapped between her thighs, sitting quietly before her buckets of greens. Angelita who just sits there and never even bother to call out to anybody to come and buy from her; her beauty just draw them and they come and buy her fresh greens that she and her father grow. Now Golden Days comes up to her, he stops singing and asks what he always asks:

"How much for the dollar bundle of callaloo?"

And Angelita smiles and says:

"One dollar fifty."

Golden Days bent down in one smooth movement like you fold a hinged object and he is looking into her eyes now:

"How much you say for the one-dollar bundle of callaloo?"

Angelita blushes and smiles:

"I say one dollar fifty."

Soon after Golden Days left the market a big commotion broke out. Two police jeeps filled with Harman Barracks men draw up outside the market. Then the police and soldier rush over to the fish section and started to turn over the fish carts and at that moment the market turned into a sea for

Angelita. Honestly, it's like she found herself under the ocean and all the people in the market began to look like fish fluttering up and down. The women in bright dresses and head ties and aprons looked like parrot fish and butter fish and the men could be doctor fish and the fat fish man could be a grouper and Angelita hurrying toward the market gate with small quick steps was, of course, an angelfish.

The next day she heard from people in the market that the police uncovered two submachine guns in Pappa Tappa's cart, well wrapped in newspaper and plastic. Pappa Tappa said he had no idea how they had reached into his cart, and the police said he should come with them to Harman Barracks and see if he could remember.

Something always happened when Golden Days pass through. When Angelita thought about it, she wondered if Golden Days was a science man.

One morning she woke up and made tea for her father as usual. Normally he was up just five a.m. but today he was still lying in bed at six-thirty, so she brought the tea to him in bed. He took it from her and said, "I don't feel so good." So she said maybe he should take some cerasee tea instead of the green tea she had made him, and he said no, he would drink the green tea.

Angelita's father was quite old, but most mornings he was up watering the callaloo and pak choi and feeding the chickens: but this day he stayed inside all day lying in his single bed covered up under a sheet, just singing feebly to himself. So Angelita fed the chickens and watered the greens and worked in the yard all that day. She killed a chicken and made soup for her father, but he barely drank a little. Next day it was the same thing.

Angelita told her father to make her take him to the doctor. He said no, but drank some cerasee tea that evening. That night, in the middle of the night, she woke up because her father was snoring so loudly. She got up to turn him over. Before she could do it, it seemed somebody else had turned him over and the snoring cut off sharp. Angelita screamed out into the night.

After the funeral, Angelita did not know what to do except to go on living like she'd always lived when her father was alive. She was his only child and her mother died when she was a baby. The small one-roomed house they had shared was on a little piece of captured land. Everybody who lived there was a squatter. They all moved closer to Angelita for a while after the funeral, but somehow she preferred to be on her own. The men tried to get her more than ever, so she had to sleep with her bed up against the door and to read Psalm 4 every night. Also she believed her father's spirit was looking after her, she kept seeing him in her mind standing up straight like a soldier outside the door of their little house. Funny thing about Angelita, she relied very much on the pictures in her mind to tell her what to do. Like when she wanted to know if something was right for her to do, she would wait and see if a picture of a lavender flower came into her mind. If she thought to do something and the lavender flower came into her mind, then she would know it was all right to do it.

She thought in pictures a lot, there was so much inside her that she saw, she sometimes wondered if she was "quiet mad" – like how she had seen the market turn into a sea when the policemen came and turned over the cart. Angelita kept these things to herself in case people thought she was really mad. She didn't talk a lot because the world in her head was so much prettier than what was around her. Like she always saw herself with a really special man. Nobody in her surroundings was good enough. She knew people say that Indian women were supposed to be very hot-blooded, well, she had never been overcome by passion for any of the men around her. Angelita had a vision of herself living in a nice big pink and white house with a man whom she did not recognize in her dreams, none of the men she knew looked like that.

One night before she fell asleep it occurred to her that she had not seen Golden Days for some time. And the next day she saw him. She heard him first, across the market, his singing seemed to be coming directly at her. It's like he was surrounding her with his singing and her head felt light and she felt light, her whole body was like it was lifted up by his singing. Then the crowd before her just parted and Golden Days was standing before her. He came up to her and he was still singing and the sound of his singing made her feel lighter, and lighter, then he bent down in the one smooth movement, like you fold something with well-oiled hinges, and still singing said to her (dropping his voice soft, soft), he said:

"Angel, I hear you father gone and you have nobody now? Is true, Angel?"

And Angelita, who was accustomed to keeping her feelings to herself, started to cry, right there in the market. It's the most she had cried since her father's death.

"Baby girl, cry, you will feel better," said Golden Days. But Angelita did not feel better, she wanted to do more than cry, she wanted to let out some of all that was inside her, to share her secret world with somebody else.

"Leave your load a little and come make me and you go for a walk."

He turned to the woman sitting across from Angelita:

"Watch her bundle for her no, Miss B, she don't feel so good."

And before Angelita could think of saying anything, the lavender flower just opened up inside her head. She went with Golden Days, out through the market and she walked and talked and cried and she never went back to the market that day.

She found out that Golden Days was a dreamer too and that freed her to tell him all about the things that went on inside her. Golden Days understood.

His dreams had to do with music. One day he was going to be a big-time ballad singer. He wanted to sing mainly love songs, he did not want to sing any dance-hall music and slackness. And Angelita told him how she wanted to live in a pink and white house and grow flowers, not callaloo and pak choi and that she hated the smell of chickens. The only thing Golden Days wondered about was how they were going to manage because he wanted a gold house. Then she thought some more and said:

"Maybe a pink and gold house?"

Golden Days's dreams of becoming a great ballad singer did not go well although he had a beautiful voice. When he sang "You'll Never Walk Alone" or "I Believe" at any stage show, the crowd would go wild. But as far as recording was concerned, what people were buying was slackness. Some deejays and singers made fortunes off singing lyrics that say some things about women that would make anybody feel ashamed of their own mother. But that was what the public was buying right now.

Golden Days said his heart and conscience could never give him to sing any songs like that. Angelita hated the slack music too. She saw their match as the first step toward living a clean and pretty life; no, no slackness for Golden Days and Angelita.

At first there was a magic quality to life with Golden Days. He had moved into the little room with her, but first he fixed it up. He painted the walls with some cheap white paint and then he bought a child's paintbox. He painted Angelita's hands and feet with different colours and made her press them all over the walls. She made a patchwork quilt by going down to a garment factory and getting a bunch of "scrapses" cheap and the little room was cozy and glowing with colour and love. It was not a pink and gold house, it was more like a jewelled cave.

But things got harder and harder and plenty of days if Angelita did not sell some greens, no pot would bubble on the fire. Angelita began to wonder what Golden Days really did every day when he left the yard to go to the studio with his exercise book of songs. He began to lose weight. Sometimes he picked up a little painting job here and there. Almost a year went by and Angelita began to wonder if he was really ever going to make it. Then one day a producer saw Golden Days outside the studio gate, he remembered him from seeing him on a Christmas morning stage show at the Carib Theatre. The producer said he had just the song for a voice like Golden Days's, it was called "Slackness Goes Cultural" and it was a new and nasty set of lyrics done to the tune of "You'll Never Walk Alone." Golden Days shook his head; the producer took out his wallet. Golden Days remembered Angelita and how sad she looked as she was still cleaning out the chicken coop, how the corners of her pretty mouth turned down, as they were no nearer to realizing the dream of the pink and gold house and he said to the producer, "Let me see it."

That night when he went home he was very quiet, and just before he fell asleep he said to Angelita, "I cut a tune today, you know."

And she said (as if she knew):

"What kind a tune?"

And he didn't answer her for a long time. Then across the darkness in the little room came Golden Days's voice, but not the rich strong one that had such power over Angelita, this voice was low and thin. Instead of making her feel excited, brushed by fingers of gentle lightning, it made her feel sick and anxious. He said:

"The song slack, well slack too, but the money is for you."

Angelita never answered. She turned her back to him and closed her eyes tight tight, because she knew they were losing something she did not want to lose.

From that time, Golden Days began to look to her ordinary, even pathetic sometimes, and it was funny because the song became a great dance-hall hit and Golden Days became very popular, even as Angelita became more and more repulsed by him.

The room they shared did not look like a magic cave anymore, it looked like pickney foolishness and she really didn't feel proud when other people asked her if it was her boyfriend who sang "Slackness Goes Cultural." Golden Days realized that Angelita had turned away from him; but suddenly there were a lot of other women, pretty uptown girls who were checking him after he did stage shows, women who just loved to hear the slackness. Angelita began to find that she couldn't bear it now when he put his hands on her. Eventually he began to go away on foreign tours for months at a time, leaving her alone there in the big pink and gold house that he built for them when he began making bushels of money after he became the slackest singer in Jamaica.

Shilling

S HE KNEW they had begun to call her Shilling. One after-
noon as she was making her way past the group of boys
congregated outside the Cross Roads post office, one of the
boys took a shilling from his pocket, came up to her, and said,
"I hear that you cost one shilling."

Shilling was a slim, fair-skinned girl and we all knew that
she was "bad," that she slept with boys, that she went to night-
clubs, and that is why she was always falling asleep in class.
Last term, Shilling had dyed her hair jet-black, bleached it
blonde, dyed it red, very red, light brown, dark brown. Every
week she changed the colour of her hair, till the headmistress
had spoken in assembly about girls who made themselves look
cheap and vulgar by dying their hair every colour of the rain-
bow; girls, who, it seems, could not even comport themselves
with a modicum of dignity as befitting a young woman who
was fortunate enough to have gained admittance to our illus-
trious school that was founded over one hundred years ago by
the Church of England with the expressed purpose of turning

out refined and useful young women. Headmistress said if such girls did not cease and desist their common behaviour, she would encourage such girls to avail themselves of the educational opportunities offered elsewhere. You had to give it to headmistress, she would never ever just say that if Shilling did not stop dyeing her hair, she would expel her from school.

Actually, Shilling was given the name not because of what vicious and untruthful schoolgirls and boys said about her selling herself for a shilling, it was because she had dyed her hair an extraordinary shade of platinum blonde that had turned kind of green, and Helen, the school wit, had said that her hair had the appearance of a gangrenous shilling.

It seemed she wanted to change herself so badly. Up until last term she had been a quiet, dreamy, not-so-bright girl, then in one term she became the notorious Shilling.

Shilling knew no one would believe her, that up until last term she was as innocent as the most innocent girl in the school, certainly more innocent than a lot of them.

That all she ever wanted was to get through fifth form, get a job, maybe in a bank, meet a nice man, marry, and have babies. That was the extent of her ambition. There were teachers predicting that some girls were going to be great scientists like Marie Curie and others were going to be great leaders of society; all Shilling ever wanted was to get married and have some babies. She used to draw her wedding dress in class all the time and cancel her name with the name of whichever boy she had a crush on at the time. She designed elaborate gowns trimmed with lace, which she drew as loops around the hem, around the sleeves, travelling up and down the bodice of these dream wedding dresses. She always drew herself with a long veil covering her face, because she was going to be a virgin when she got married. She would also draw her "change" dress, or going-away dress, the dress in which she would go off to her honeymoon, that's all she ever wanted and in good order.

Then she fell in love with him. She saw him at a Manning cup match. He was dark and not too tall and he had the most unusual face, large dark eyes, and a nose with a slight hump in the middle like a boxer. He moved very lightly when he walked, which was unusual for a football player; he moved more like a dancer. She took one look at him sitting there in the grandstand with his arm around his girlfriend's chair and she fell in love, absolutely and fatally, the way only a sixteen-year-old girl could fall in love. Somehow it did not seem to matter to her that he was sitting with his arm around his girlfriend's chair. Her eyes registered the girl, but she did not care; all she saw was him. The girl was very stuck-up-looking, boasy, and conceited, she thought. She had good skin and a pretty-enough face, but she looked heavy, like she was of the earth; you couldn't imagine her dreaming about flying as Shilling so often dreamt, that she grew wings and was flying to see her mother in New York. She was a very confident girl, though, confident of her relationship with him. And anybody but Shilling could see that he thought the sun and moon resided in this girl and rose and set only when she gave them permission. When the peanut man came around with his song that always made schoolboys and girls laugh – "Mi say just done bake and them sweeter than a cake, a so them criss, mi say a no teet miss . . ." – everyone laugh except his girlfriend. She just told him to get her some peanuts and he jumped over three rows of seats to get them. When he came back, he sat down and shelled the peanuts for her; she held out her palm and received them as her due. Shilling never watched the match, she just watched him shelling peanuts for this girl and the girl accepting them by sticking her palm out sideways and never even saying thank you, just looking at the match and eating the peanuts when her palm was full enough. Shilling thought to herself, What an awful girl, what does he see in her; if it were her, she would have been shelling the peanuts for him. When the match was over, he took his blazer from the empty seat next to him and draped it across her shoulders like a queenly cape. She just accepted it as her due, sort of shrugged her shoulders into it, and then they walked hand in hand from the grandstand through the tunnel out of the stadium.

She asked a boy she knew who went to his school, and he told her his name. She asked about the girlfriend and the guy told her the girlfriend was wealthy, she drove her own car, and that everyone thought she was very full of herself and that the boy in question came from a poor but decent family and the girlfriend "had him soft," everybody knew that.

The next week, she saw him at a bus stop; he was standing with some other boys, one of whom she knew. She made sure she passed close to him and made sure that he saw her; she felt so thrilled just to be near him, just to walk across his shadow. When she saw the boy she knew, she asked for an introduction to him. Of course the boy told him because the next time she saw him and his girlfriend, the girl looked at her and laughed out loud, then whispered something to him and he just grinned. But she didn't care, she was absolutely in love with him. She cancelled his name with hers, she tried to divine his presence into her life by a schoolgirl's mystic and romantic mathematics. Add up all the numbers on your bus ticket, then match the final number to this rhyme: one for sorrow, two for joy, three for girl, four for boy, five for silver, six for gold, seven for a secret that's never been told. She always seemed to be getting seven, not four for boy as she hoped.

Her wedding dresses became more elaborate, and now she drew him beside her as the groom. She tried to draw his boxer's nose and his deep eyes. And she began to imagine every detail of the ceremony. How she would walk up the aisle to Patti LaBelle and the Bluebelles singing "Down the Aisle"; how she would promise to love and honour and, yes, obey him; how they would drive away in a car marked "Just Married"; and how he would crush his lips passionately to hers . . . just like in a Mills & Boon romance. She was so absorbed in this dream that she began to get into bad trouble at school for daydreaming and inattention. Once, the geography teacher came up behind her as she was drawing a particularly ornate wedding dress. The teacher snatched the drawing out of her hand and ridiculed her before the class, told her that in order to get married she would need a groom and that men were not fond of useless women; that she was useless, stupid, and good for nothing. She then gave her her two hundred lines to write after school: "I am not a bride and the classroom is not a chapel. I must work hard and study Geography while I am in Geography class." Two hundred lines.

When Shilling left detention, it was quite late and she missed seeing him at the bus stop.

She began to go to every Manning cup football match in which he played, to go to every school function where she might see him. She was boarding with a family as her mother was in New York working, so she told them lies to explain why she came in late every evening. She had Science club, and Bible Knowledge group, and netball practice after school, and rehearsals for plays that never took place. She did not care; all she wanted was to be anyplace where he was.

Then Donna A. had her sweet-sixteenth birthday party. She was not a close friend, but she was invited to the party. The truth is, Donna wanted to get as many presents as possible; the girls had a competition, to see who could have the most elaborate sweet-sixteen party, who could get the most presents. One girl had received six of the same Desert Flower hand lotion and cologne sets, four bottles of Blue Grass cologne, and at least ten handkerchief sets, two baby doll pyjamas, and fourteen boxes of Cadbury chocolate from one party. Shilling was very happy to attend because Donna told her that he would be there, with his girlfriend, yes, but he would be there.

Her mother sent her from New York a blue satin dress. The skirt was shaped like a bell and there was a large artificial rose to one side of the skirt. She thought it was a beautiful dress, and that she looked lovely, very grown-up in it. But the moment when she saw him arrive with his girlfriend she felt like a child. He was dressed like all the other boys in a dark suit, white shirt, and tie, but his girlfriend was in a white chiffon dress, close-fitting and low-cut. They looked like the perfect couple; when they entered the room everybody turned to look at them. They danced only with each other. Both sides of the Drifters LP. Up on the roof, you only dance with somebody to two sides of a Drifters LP if you had practically pledged your life to them. You would stand wrapped in each other's arms, hardly moving from that one spot, and rent a tile into happiness.

Eventually some sweating boy asked her to dance and she manoeuvred him close to where they were dancing together tight as two five cents in a ten cent. No breeze could blow between them, eyes closed, moving as one body.

Shilling closed her eyes, moved closer to the sweating boy who was her partner, transporting herself across the dance floor into his arms. It was really her, Shilling, he was dancing with, not Miss High-and-Mighty in the white chiffon dress. Then Miss High-and-Mighty boxed him. Right there on the dance floor. One minute they were the perfect couple, then, who knows what she said to him or him to her and what the reply was, but she slapped him just like some woman in a movie and walked off the dance floor, leaving him standing there looking like a fool. Everybody stopped dancing and began asking what the matter was, and he was just looking stunned and holding his face, and she was just pushing her way out across the veranda, down through the yard, jangling the keys to her car. Then he ran after her.

For a while everybody stood talking about what happened. Then they settled down again to enjoy the party. Shilling kept telling everyone how she thought the girl was dreadful. Most people said yes, but he was just totally in love with her so he would put up with anything. About an hour later he came back to the party without her. When everybody started to ask him what was the matter, he refused to answer. He just went over to the bar where he stood for a long while drinking beer after beer and not saying anything. Shilling just sat and watched him. Then he walked over to her and held out his hand; he didn't say a word, he was so sure of her response. Shilling went right to him, he pulled her close, and they danced for a long while. He never said anything; she felt sweat (or tears) running down his cheek and he kept his eyes shut tight.

Shilling never used to dance really close with anybody, but now she was pasted right up against him. She was so happy, she was trembling. It was a good thing they hardly moved or she would never have followed his steps. She was in his arms!

Later in the night he spoke. He said, "Come with me," and she followed him round to the back of the house where there was an empty room. It looked like an abandoned maid's quarters, a single bed with an old beat-up mattress and a little broken locker. He took her there, laid her down on the mattress, and with great force and no tenderness emptied his humiliation into her. He never even called her darling or asked how she was, nothing, but she was glad to be there for him; now he would probably realize which girl really loved him. She opened her eyes, which were screwed tight with the pain and shock and happiness and hope, and that is when she saw the other boys standing in the room.

Talola's Husband

⁓

IN TRUTH, the wedding was not what my mother would call a "big splash"; for though it was held in the evening, Talola wore a dress that looked like it was once somebody else's long wedding gown that she had cut short. The ornate guipure lace on the dress had gone a deep off-white and, in order to give the dress a fresh look, she had stitched a frill round the neckline made from a different patterned, newer lace. It was as if she was wearing something old and something new on the same dress.

Also, the rice and peas and chicken ran out before all the guests had been served, but her husband looked like a high official sitting there at the wedding table, which was spread with my mother's white damask tablecloth decorated at the four corners with asparagus ferns and shaggy-haired pink asters. Only a modest two-storey wedding cake and a lone cut-glass decanter of dark red wine graced the centre of the table; still, the groom, dressed as he was in an elegant but slightly rusty-looking blue serge suit, rose and stood with his chest thrown out, as if he were presiding over a royal banquet, when it was time for him to reply on behalf of him and his bride.

"Ladies and gentlemen, I am chuffed that this esteemed and assembled gathering has congregated here upon this, my nuptial day, to partake of potations and libations." Everybody said, "Speech, speech" and "Word outta book" because of the eloquence of his presentation. Every time I saw him thereafter he was very well turned out, usually in dark trousers with a white or a blue shirt, and sometimes he even wore a jacket. His shoes were highly polished and he always wore or carried a black felt hat.

"Mr. Harold Harrington to see the lady of the house." That is how he would announce himself when he came to visit us. He would then remove his black felt hat and hold it gingerly by the rim with his fingertips or balance it delicately on one knee for the rest of his visit.

"A gentleman never wears his hat inside a house." When I told my father that Talola's new husband had said this, he said the man was not a gentleman, and the only reason he was allowed inside our house was because he'd married my mother's distant cousin.

"Talola." I liked her name. Sometimes I said it over and over just to feel it roll back and forth across my tongue. Talola did not look like her glamorous name. She was a short, round-faced, squinty-eyed woman who chainsmoked Buccaneer cigarettes until her index and middle fingers were stained a reddish yellow, as if she varnished cabinets for a living. Her husband's index and middle fingers were also remarkable, for they were of the same length. My brothers told me that it was because he had stretched the joints of his index finger until it became as long as his middle finger. They said he did that so he could insert them like tongs into people's pockets and pinch up their wallet. They said that was all that Talola's husband did while he was in prison, day and night. He just kept pulling at the joints of his right index finger until it became as long as his middle finger.

My father said that Mr. Harrington's good manners were directly attributable to the influence of the then-superintendent of prisons, an Englishman named Cornwall, who had taken a liking to the handsome young man when he was serving his first sentence. Superintendent Cornwall, according to my father, had taken on the young Harrington as a project to prove that nurture, not nature, could shape the soul and spirit of a man. What Harrington seemed to have learned from Cornwall was how not to wear your hat inside of a house, how to recite poetry and speak so sweetly that you could samfie country people into buying land in the Kingston Race Course, and get them to lend you money to keep attending the funeral of your mother whose heart had given way ten years ago because her son would not stop bringing down disgrace upon her.

On my thirteenth birthday, I learned something from Talola. I was trying to cook dinner because my mother said to me that morning:

"You are now of an age where you should be able to handle yourself in the kitchen."

Obviously she thought that I had served enough apprenticeship doing small tasks like cutting up seasoning for meat and picking small black stones and other foreign bodies from rice. So there I was trying to remember that you could put yellow yams into cold water, but you had to drop green bananas into boiling water. That you should always add a piece of salted cod fish to attract the stain of the soft-boiling green bananas – a stain that becomes dark and pervasive once the bananas come in contact with the boiling water and can coat all the food in the pot with murky indigo scum (the salt fish acts as a sort of stain/scum magnet).

I was trying to judge just how much salt to use when I seasoned the meat, for in our house there was no such thing as measuring when it came to cooking; I was trying to remember all this culinary wisdom when I burnt my hand on the side of the iron Dutch pot. Talola, who was visiting us, came into the kitchen to see what I was bawling about and said:

"Put your hand right back near to the fire."

Before I could ask her if she was crazy, she grabbed my hand and brought it right up close to the flames and held it there. I do not know how to explain this, but after a while it seemed as if the terrible burning leapt out of my hand and went back into the fire. I have tried this on other occasions and sometimes it works and sometimes it does not, but I swear that that day it worked. I began to like Talola for more than just her name after that, and I began to feel sorry for her when she came to tell my mother about her husband's latest act of skulduggery.

"Cousin Dor, Saturday gone you nearly hear say you poor cousin Talola gone to workshouse. I was in the kitchen cooking a pot of pumpkin soup for Mr. Harrington dinner (she always called him Mr. Harrington) when I see him fly through the gate, and run into the kitchen, and quick quick drop something into the pot, then fly inside the room, tear off him shirt, and lie down on the bed in him merino. Not five minutes after that, police burst through the gate looking for him, say him pick a man pocket by the bus stop. Hear him:

"'Officer, what is this commotion about? I must protest that you are disturbing my afternoon rest. I have been lying here for the past hour in vacant and in pensive mood waiting on my good wife, Mrs. Talola Harrington, to serve me some of her Saturday soup.'

"Seeing as how him was only a blue-seam policeman who not too long come from the country, and who never hear word like that coming out of a black man mouth, the policeman turn fool and just stand up just a look like him lost. The wallet was nowhere in sight when the policeman stir himself and search up Mr. Harrington and the room. The policeman go through the gate a shake him head. And, you know, after him gone, Mr. Harrington fish the wallet out of the pot, take out the two pound that was in it, spread them to dry on the windowsill and drink the soup! Hear him: 'After all, this is a leather wallet, so this has become cowskin soup. I couldn't eat cousin, I smoke about ten pack of cigarette since Saturday.'"

Talola concluded her story with a round of rapid-fire coughing.

After a time Mr. H had to stop picking pockets because his presence was so outstanding. My mother said that as a child he had shown great promise as an athlete, and that if he had any ambition at all he could have been a runner like the great Jamaican Arthur Wint, but Mr. H had one true calling and everybody knew what that was.

He took next to specializing in hole-in-the roof robberies, and here he truly excelled. Leaping effortlessly from roof to roof, his long legs carrying him in swift, swooping motions, his bag of loot suspended over his shoulder, his jacket filled with the night wind, his cat's eyes penetrating the darkness. He would leap, then land on his feet, crouch, and leap again until he was far away. The police had difficulty catching him, so they harassed Talola instead.

Talola came to our house early one morning and made no move to go home even when it was past ten o'clock. My mother finally told her that she could sleep in the backroom as the last bus had already left. I went to sleep worrying that the police would come and arrest our entire family during the night.

My mother said that Talola met Mr. Harrington when she was working in a hardware store on Princess Street. She was alone in the little shop one day when Mr. H had burst in and asked her to allow him to use the toilet as he was having an emergency. Talola took one look at the very handsome, distinguished-looking brown man and pointed him to the small water closet behind the shop. A minute or so later, some people yelling, "Thief! Thief!" ran past. Mr. Harrington emerged after about half an hour and thanked Talola profusely for allowing him the use of her "comfort station." Talola did notice that he was then wearing a shirt of a different colour. Later she would find out that he needed to have at least two clean shirts every day because he always wore more than one in case he needed to make a quick change. She noticed too that he arranged to stand so that he was hidden from the street by several tall rolls of linoleum for the entire time that he stood in the shop. But he also looked to her that day like a great orator standing before the Ionic columns of some important building, focusing his gold-green eyes on her face, giving a speech meant for her ears only, about what a fine and generous woman she was to save him from embarrassment by allowing him the use of her sanitary convenience.

Talola brought him good luck, for after he took up with her he hardly ever got caught. She on the other hand developed her horrible rattling cough because she, who prior to meeting Harrington had been a hard-working store clerk who had lived at the same address for seventeen years, began a series of hasty moves from one end of the city of Kingston to the other. She invariably moved by night, her fine mahogany dresser and bed heaped hastily onto some crude handcart as she fled with her beloved from the police or from one of his irate victims.

No amount of aromatic camphor, slimy bitter aloes, sooty lamp oil, or garlic could cure Talola's cough. To cure it, Talola even tried cutting down on her cigarettes, which were a form of nourishment to her because she claimed they kept her nerves steady, but her cough kept rattling like dice in a leather ludo cup.

"Talola, you better go and see a doctor," my mother told her.

And then there was the "She was a phantom of delight" incident that involved Mr. Harrington and my sister one day when she, who was one of the best-dressed young women in the city of Kingston thanks to my mother's peerless dress-making, encountered him on King Street.

The incident occurred when my fabulous sister was about to ascend to the top floor of Nathan's Department Store, there to lunch with a group of her fine friends, when she saw Mr. Harrington bearing down on her. She tried to pretend that she had not seen him, but he pressed forward through the crowd, threw his arms around her, and planted a big kiss on her cheek.

"She was a phantom of delight, when first she graced my sight," quoth he as she stood there wishing that King Street would open up and swallow her. Everyone in our family blamed my mother for this incident because she always treated Mr. Harrington like a normal person. My father said that if my mother had not insisted on entertaining the thieving son of a bitch, then my parents' beloved first-born child would not have been embarrassed in that way. We did not see either Talola or Mr. Harrington for some time after that.

Then one day my mother got a telephone call from one of her many relatives, who told her that Talola had been diagnosed with lung cancer. A few weeks later she got another call that Talola had died. When my parents came back from the funeral they told us how Mr. H had bawled like a baby, and that Talola had been buried in her wedding dress, and I cried when I heard that because I found the image romantic.

The next time that we heard about Mr. H was when we read a headline in the afternoon paper: "CRIMINAL CASTIGATED BY CAUSTIC COUNSEL." It seemed that Mr. H had tried to pull off another daring hole-in-the-roof robbery, but it being so soon after Talola's death, his heart must have been weighted with grief. This time he did not swoop like a long-legged predator from roof to roof and, instead of landing lightly on his feet and crouching then springing forward again, he dropped heavily between two buildings and his long legs snapped like sticks. When they brought him into court on two crutches, the judge showed him no sympathy. He said that a fine-looking and articulate man like Mr. H had no business coming before the courts for burglary. Just before he sentenced him to three years' hard labour, he threatened that if he ever saw him in court again he would put him away for a very long time.

One Sunday, we were sitting down to dinner when we heard those courtly words: "Mr. Harold Harrington to see the lady of the house."

"O God," said my father. My mother, who treated every visitor, no matter how humble and mean their station, as an honoured guest, said, "The Bible says we should not be forgetful to entertain strangers: for thereby some have entertained angels unawares."

"I know of the angel of mercy, so I guess this man must be the angel of larceny," said my father.

Ignoring that remark, she got up from the table and went outside and greeted Mr. Harrington. She came back in, fixed him some dinner, and took it to him on a tray. We then heard him say, "I indeed intend to go straight down to Heywood Street and catch a bus to the country where I still have some relatives, and thank you, my dear lady, for these five shillings."

But his move to the country did not work out, for the last time we ever heard anything of him was when we read this headline: "COOL-HEADED FELON FOILED," in the *Star* newspaper. It seems that Mr. Harrington had indeed tried to go straight, for he had gotten a regular job in a meat-processing factory, but one day he just could not resist the urge to hide a pack of frozen chicken parts under his hat. When the watchman demanded that he remove his head-gear as he went out through the factory gates, Mr. H protested that he was no longer indoors, and that the rules of proper etiquette allowed a gentleman to keep his hat on outdoors. The guard, a man who preferred to eat his food straight from the pot with the aid of a broad-mouthed spoon, was underwhelmed.

Alice and the Dancing Angel

❧

"AND NOW, fresh from St. Thomas, the parish of our national heroes, we present to you the Sexy Scotch Bonnet, hotter than a bird pepper, jerk seasoning, or pickapeppa, sweet like a sweetpepper, cool black and comely like the Queen of Sheba . . . Aliiiice."

No Alice.

When the emcee stepped behind the piece of plyboard that divided the front stage from the back he saw Alice lying down, stretched out as if a duppy had boxed her.

Alice had been waiting in the wings at the Front and Centre Club on Red Hills Road to perform her Sexy Scotch Bonnet act in her plaid bandana G-string, her raffia brassiere, and her wide cartwheel of a jippi-jappa hat without a crown when an angel stepped in. The angel took up a position right in front of the stage among the cheering throng of die-hard fans and supporters of Kitty and Katty. Nobody else seemed to notice its presence but Alice, who was peeping from behind the plyboard partition trying to figure out what scorching scotch bonnet moves she could make to hold the howling, horny audience when her turn came.

The first thing that registered with Alice was that the angel was black. He looked like a black man – that is, if an angel can be called a man. She could not see his face distinctly because something about the size of a quarter-yard or so of moonlight was obscuring its head. The seraph had on a long royal-blue gown with a broad yellow stripe running around the hem. There were two big, stiff, well-feathered wings growing out of his shoulder blades and he kept shrugging his shoulders, moving the wings backward and forward in perfect time to the music.

Alice gave out a loud scream, but Shabba Ranks was growling from the belly of the sound system and the men in the bar were howling concupiscent encouragement to Kitty and Katty, who were hard into their sexy twin kittens dance so that no one heard when Alice screamed.

Kitty and Katty, two half-Syrian girls, were the latest, hottest act at the club. Men were coming from all over Jamaica just to see these identical twins bump and grind in synchron-ized movement. Their act always brought the house down, so when Alice gave out a loud "Lord, have mercy" no one was paying her any attention.

Kitty and Katty left the stage and undulated into the steamy crowd to execute some lucrative lap dancing while the emcee rubbed down Alice with some white rum till she rallied. She kept pointing to the place where the angel was, but nobody else could see anything like what Alice was trying to describe. They all concluded that her head had taken her or that she had taken some bad drugs. Mrs. Cameron, the owner of the club who always insisted on being called Mrs. Cameron and was forever reminding people "I am a big married woman," told Alice that she should go home. "As a matter of fact," she said, "please consider leaving the job altogether because I do not want to be the one to have to commit you to Bellevue, for I'm a big married woman."

Mrs. Cameron had never really liked Alice, she never understood her. The girl could really dance but she always had a lost, faraway look. "She goes on as if she is better than me, a big married woman."

After a while Alice got up and washed her face and slowly put on her street clothes and walked outside to catch a bus on Red Hills Road. While she was standing at the bus stop, the angel appeared beside her and stood rocking back and forth. Alice started to bawl out and the angel wheeled around, laid a forefinger over her lips, then leapt straight up into the air and disappeared.

When the bus arrived it was surprisingly not full. Alice got in and paid the conductor. When she glanced behind her the angel was right there. The bus moved off, and after a while everybody on the bus began to talk softer. Even a drunken man who was telling everybody about how the prime minister used to come to him to write his speeches.

"And that is the reason why the prime minister's speeches sounding so sheg-up these days, because he and I had a falling out over certain matters, which I can't talk about on this bus, but suffice it to say, these matters involve a woman."

Even he fell silent eventually, and Alice noticed that
the angel was gently rocking back and forth right behind
the driver, who then began to drive at a fairly reasonable
pace. Once or twice, to her amazement, he even stopped to
give the right of way to cars from side roads. When the bus
pulled up downtown, Alice came off and the angel stepped
off right behind her. Alice picked up the pace, hoping to
lose the heavenly being in the crowd, but every time she
looked around it was still right behind her. Alice picked up
foot and ran but when she looked up, the angel was floating
right above her head like a gas balloon.

She collided with a man who was selling curtain rods
and hangers, and she and the man both tumbled down in
the street.

Alice started to cry. No, it would be fair to say that Alice
started to bawl. She bawled so loudly that the curtain rod
man asked her:

"What happen, is a little bounce make you a gwan so?"

Alice could not explain. She was just crying and looking
up at the angel floating above her head. She prostrated her-
self face down on the sidewalk and hollered. The women
who were passing all came to the exact same conclusion.

"No mind, my dear. Don't make him mad you."

"Suppose you did have my baby father to deal with, what
you would do?"

"No mind, mi dear. Don't make man mad you."

"Suppose you did have my husband to deal with, what
you would do?"

"No mind, mi dear. Don't make man mad you."

"You can make man bring you to this? Gal, get up."

After a while Alice stopped crying and she felt a calm settle on her as if somebody had thrown a bridal veil over her face and head and a nice little breeze was just blowing through it. She got up off the sidewalk and began to walk to where she lived. This time she didn't look behind her, beside her, or above her. She just walked straight, and when she reached the gate of her yard she made a quick dash inside, opened the door to her room, jumped inside, and dropped the bolt behind her.

Neither Miss Dulce nor Kenisha was in the room. Miss Dulce was the rum-head woman to whom Alice paid a smalls to watch Kenisha for her on the nights when she worked. Alice figured that maybe Miss Dulce had to go to the shop to buy rum because she couldn't find where Alice had hidden her bottle of bay rum or her perfume, both of which she had been known to sip when she was out of white rum, and she had taken Kenisha with her. Alice lay down on her bed, wrung out from all the excitement and the angel appearance and the fainting and the prostration and the crying. Alice had not cried in years.

Alice closed her eyes and she began to hear some really sweet pipe organ music. It reminded her of when she was a child in Morant Bay and she used to dress up in her organdy dress on a Sunday and go for a walkout by the seaside and eat fudge and icicle. On those Sundays she would sometimes go with her friends to look at the statue of Paul Bogle in front of the courthouse. Alice remembers that one time she danced before the statue just to see if Deacon Paul would come alive and put down his machete that he was holding before him like a cross.

"The little girl who can dance," that is what everybody in the town of Morant Bay called her. That is why, after she had won every medal in the annual Festival Dance competition, she had come to Kingston to go to the School of Dance with the intention of going back to Morant Bay as a dance teacher. Alice still can't quite figure out how she has ended up doing go-go dancing at the Front and Centre Club. She can't figure out how she has ended up with three children from different fathers, and right here so now, with an angel in a blue gown outside her room door, she really, really does not want anybody, I mean anybody at all, to ask her any question about how she reached where she reached.

Don't forget yourself and send any more children to me, for the two Kingston-born wretches that you send here are sending me to an early grave. She had sent the first two children to stay with her mother in the country. Her mother had sent her that message when she had written to her about the impending birth of Kenisha.

She got up out of the bed, opened the door, and stepped outside to go and look for her daughter. "Please help me find my daughter Kenisha," she called out into the dark, as if the angel was hard of hearing. As she said that, she felt it lift her up and rise up with her swiftly over the gate.

The view from above was very different than when you were walking on the street. While the angel was carrying Alice she could look down into other people's yards and see all of the yard, like pictures in a frame. She could see long stretches of street, and it occurred to her that streets were laid out in a perfect pattern like bandana plaid, with streets going across and streets going down.

The funny thing was she was not really frightened. As a matter of fact, she never felt so very secure in her life. However, she still could not make out the features of the angel because the glow veil was still covering its face. The mighty winged being began its descent when they approached a cross street where a dance was going on. A smoke cloud rose up to them as they reached the corner where there were about a hundred people at a street dance at a venue known as Yasso Yasso. Alice looked down and immediately she could make out Miss Dulce in a bundle of much younger women. Dulce was trying to outwine them. She was also smoking what looked like a spliff. Must be a seasoned weed spliff because ganja alone could not be making Dulce be going on so. She was bending down and spreading out so much that she was sure to injure some vital part of her seventy-year-old body. Alice's eyes swept past Dulce, looking for Kenisha, whom she finally spotted lying like a cloth doll on a beer box in a corner.

If on any other night Alice had come across this same scene, she would have joined in. And as a bona fide wining practitioner, she would have shown them some professional moves. Or she would have just taken up Kenisha and gone home, depending on how the spirit moved her. But tonight, from her angel's eye view, she just wanted to weep at the sight of her small girl child lying down on a beer box on the road side. She begged the angel, "Please put me down, make me go for her."

The angel landed in the middle of the crowd right next to a don who was visiting from New York and who was attired in a pink, crushed-velvet, juicy track suit, generously accessorized by gold chains, one of which was carefully crafted to be an exact replica of the necklace worn by the mayor of Kingston on state occasions.

The don was standing with one Fila-shod foot resting on his personal box of Heineken and sending up gun-salute acknowledgements every time the deejay said, "Big up, all gunman and gangster visiting from New York!"

Nobody but Alice seemed to be able to see this being in the long gown with two mighty bird wings shrugging back and forth, rocking back and forth in the midst of this crowd of people who were moving to the urgent rhythm, "Gal, yu body good yu body good o!"

The shit smell of crack cocaine was in the air.

When this deportee who was hoping that the New York don could help him to re-enter the United States tried to push his way past one of the don's bodyguards in order to get a chance to put his case personally, well, the don's bodyguard did not like that, so he shoved the boy in his chest. As he had to prove to the don that he had not lost his edge after months of living like a dog on the streets of Kingston, he who once owned a gold Lexus and lived in his own fabulous red and gold apartment in the Bronx; he who had been handcuffed early one February morning after being sold out by his Hispanic girl friend who turned out to be a DEA agent and put on a plane by U.S. Immigration and sent back to Jamaica with only the clothes on his back; he who was desperate to return to New York because he'd heard that his brother-in-law had poured sugar into the gas tank of his Lexus to mash-up the transmission; he pulled out a big knife from his waist and opened the bodyguard's cheek.

People started to fan out when the bodyguard shook his head in disbelief and blood sprinkled everyone around him. Except Alice, who at this point was pushing her way through the crowd to pick up Kenisha off the beer box. The bodyguard reached up and touched his wet face and then he did two things. He shrugged off the duffle bag that he was carrying on his shoulder and it fell at his feet. When the bag hit the pavement with a heavy dull sound, the crowd started to scatter. Then the bodyguard reached down into the bag and brought out a big gun. "Booyakka, booyakka." The deportee fluttered like a chicken. The don growled, "Strain him."

Alice had picked up Kenisha and she was trying to edge away from the corner behind the don, and the bodyguard, and the instantly dead deportee. She was trying to move away as unobtrusively as possible because she did not want her name to be called as witness.

Alice was moving in Kumina style, one foot in front of the other, doing the flat-footed Kumina shuffle. The pounding of her heart sounding in her head like the big goat-skin Kumina bass drum. She held her small daughter close to her chest, with one hand over the little girl's mouth. She is wondering where was the angel, Kumina to Kumina, thinking now is the time for it to appear, Kumina to Kumina, since he is angel, he should come now, Kumina, and lift up Alice and

Kenisha, because the bodyguard is now shaking from head to foot at the sight of the dead deportee lying at his feet. Then he turns with his face dyed with red like an ancient warrior, and like a dance-hall warrior giving his killer act a gun salute, he screams, "Respect due!" and wheels in a slow circle as he sprays bullet after bullet into the crowd.

And this is when the angel comes over and holds Alice around her waist and starts to ride the rhythm with her. He holds her tight and they hold Kenisha between them and they dance. Bogle and Tatie past the lickshot of bullets. And Alice understands then that this is her angel, the angel of dance come to wheel and turn her and her daughter past hot exploding death, to dally them safely home tonight and skank them down to the bus depot tomorrow so they can step it straight out of Killsome.

For My Comrades
Wearing Three-Piece Suits

⁓

FRIENDS AND RELATIVES stand outside on Tower Street and throw parcels over the wall at Christmastime, parcels of everything from ganja and fruitcake to cash and guns. Every time one of these packages come flying like a prison bird over the brick wall, the guard in the tower gets jumpy and fires into the air.

One week before Christmas a new warder opened up my face with a baton because I "back chat" him. They had to take me in a Black Maria down to the Kingston Public Hospital to get my face stitched up.

I saw her and although she didn't say anything I knew that she knew it was me.

She and I had exchanged enough lustful glances across the chemistry lab on campus for her to be quite familiar with my face, and that was not all that long ago.

But then again, one day a man showed me a photograph of himself that was on his driver's licence when he came in here and he did not even look like he is related to the man in the photograph. Maybe something like that has happened to me and that is why she is behaving as if she does not know me. They used to tell me that I look like Che Guevara.

The one thing that makes me feel sure she did recognize me is that she insisted that the nurse give me something to deaden the pain, even though said nurse kept saying, "You are a student doctor, so you wouldn't know that we don't usually give painkiller to prisoner."

"Just find some and give to him, please."

On the way back to prison, as we drove through downtown Kingston, I peep through the mesh wire in the Black Maria to see what outside looked like after three years, and what I see is people just freely going about their business. When I pass some youths standing up outside a bar sipping Red Stripe and skanking to the sounds from the jukebox, I would give my life to be one of them. And over and over in my head I begin to hear the words of my latest mantra, courtesy of Jimmy Cliff, "Lord, whatta price I paid. Lord, whatta price I paid." Sometimes Jimmy's sweet soaring voice just remains with me for days. Sister, what a price I paid.

My friend Patto taught me some martial arts and deep-breathing exercises. I use them to blank out the non-stop soundtrack of this horror movie directed and produced by Babylon, titled *Land of the Living Dead*. Under the rhythm of wickedness, profanity, and raw brutality is the music of the sea playing outside the brick wall. One day I saw a man run across the yard and fling himself against the wall as if he could just propel himself through the solid red brick into the salt water.

I do my deep breathing when warders say things like, "If me did have a son and me send him go a university and him turn communist and bank robber, me shoot him." I use it to block out things that have happened to me since I come in here. If Patto never taught me some of those exercises, believe me, I would be a dead man or a madman by now.

Police killed Patto one morning on Red Hills Road. Sprayed the car. Everybody in there dead including my best friend Joseph, who, as far as I know, never hurt a fly. They say we were arch-terrorists, we called ourselves revolutionaries. Fifteen years. The big veins in the judge's forehead knotted like a fist when he sentenced me to fifteen years for armed bank robbery. "Che Che Che Mao Mao Mao," that was my mantra then. I used to say that if I had a son that I would call him Stalin. Crucial crucial Stalin, that is how serious I was. Josef Stalin or Leon Trotsky.

My mother moved to Miami after the case.

"How can I live in this country after the disgrace that you bring down on my name? Nobody, nobody in my family ever tief or go to prison! Imagine some bitch saw me in the bank and come up to me and ask me how much of the stolen money you give me."

I told her: "Run, go on to Miami like your other 'gusano' friends, I don't fucking need you, my comrades are my family."

At first they would come, bringing me revolutionary books and cigarettes.

"Man, like you must get mad and rob bank when they read dem tings ya."

The guards used to love to take the books and read out loud from them – that is, the ones who could read. As for the cigarettes, plenty man in here bow over one cigarette. I am now a non-smoker.

Soap, toothpaste, toilet paper, food that a human being, as opposed to a hog, should eat. When I get any of those things they are brought by Jackson the "gardener boy" (as my mother would call the big man) and Millicent, who is more my mother than my real mother. Last Christmas, Millicent, gave me two hundred dollars. When I asked her where she get the money from as she is now only doing days' work after my mother moved to Miami and abandoned her after she had slaved for our family for twenty three years, she said, "Partner, I throw a partner for you, and this two hundred dollars is your draw."

I bribed a warder with it so I could stay down by the infirmary from Christmas to New Year and read some old *Reader's Digest*s. If you ever want to get a preview of hell, check out this place during the month of December when prisoners try to make a break for the holiday. I don't wash my face or clean my teeth from last week because it is nothing for fifteen stabbings a day to occur at the one standpipe that is supposed to serve two hundred men.

"Don't rude to me, you know say me used to gi you mi dry breast fi suck when you mother dress up and leave me fi nurse you when she gone a some cocktail party or the other. My god in heaven, you was one miserable baby."

"Jesus Christ, Millicent, you never have to tell me that!"

"You know what I did hate the most when you take up with them people is how you used to curse God."

I don't answer Millicent. The only one I am cursing these days is me. One time if she ever mentioned God's name in my presence I would automatically "blood" her.

"Don't bring any fucking Christian argument to me. Religion is the opiate of the masses."

"Lord, have mercy, him mad now!"

Millicent can barely read and write, but she is smarter than me. If I was so goddamn smart, how come I end up in here while so many of my ex-comrades are outside wearing three-piece suits? I understand that only taximan drive Lada now.

You want to hear something ridiculous? The only other person who visits me, besides Millicent and Jackson, is a Jesuit priest who comes in here to minister to the lapsed Catholics. He is a tall, thin Canadian. It's like the man has an earthquake going on inside him! He chainsmokes and shakes constantly. The first time he saw me watching him, he just said openly, "I'm an alcoholic."

"Yes? Dem say I'm a bank robber. Ahhh. Dem say."

We started laughing. Most sentences spoken in here contain the words "dem say."

"Bwoy, dem say me shat a man and him wife and pickney."

"You want see dem say me rape off this little girl."

The Canadian priest and I talk Marxism-Leninism. He has never suggested that I join his church, but he did give me this advice: "Put on the whole armour, which in this case is your education. Offer to write letters for people."

Good advice. In here, if the wicked have use for you, they might even protect you.

You know that program on RJR on Sundays, where people write in trying to find their missing relatives? At least six of the letters I write get read every week. The priest lets me use the addresses of people in his church so when you hear a letter saying, "Kenneth Brown is trying to reach his sister Catherine who used to live in Allman Town, please write to him at 50 Redwing Way, Kingston 12," this letter is really coming from a man in prison who stands a better chance of getting a reply if he does not give his address as the General Penitentiary on Tower Street.

Even the blood in my body is trying to escape through my forehead. There is a wicked and dreadful hammering behind the split between my eyes. I dig at the stitches with my dirty fingernails, my whole face might soon become one big festering sore. I want all the contaminated blood in me to burst out through this split between my eyes and gush out of my corrupted, violated, fucking idiot body, leaving only a bloodless dry skin carcass that the Tower Street breeze can just blow away like a dirty foot cloth out to sea.

Even the most psychopathic dog heart in here calls the General Penitentiary hell.

In the cells at night you piss in a gallon-sized plastic soft drink bottle, they call the bottle "yu girl." Every morning you stumble out of a stinking stopped-up hole in the wall built over one hundred years ago to accommodate men half my height, after being locked down with all form of lumpen and try to empty "yu girl." Sometimes for weeks the place is washed in sewage. This is the laboratory for breeding the island's rat, roach, bed bug, and chink.

Victims of the system. Victims of the system. At every worker's rally we said the incarcerated were just victims of the system. Believe me when I tell you that I have encountered men in here who have become little more than human rat cockroach and chink.

I read one time that in Nazi concentration camps inmates tried to hold on to their shoes. When your shoes go, then the rest of you follows. Every day I check to see if my shoes are still over the grating at the top of the cell.

When they lock me down I start to feel faint. I wake up in the infirmary. Every time I try to get up I black out. In dreams I am a Maroon warrior moving with stealth through the high green bush of Portland. Last night I feel as if my "soul" or some part of me escaped with great force through the cut in my face. I spend all night outside, my body flying across the skies over the city of Kingston. Near morning I re-enter myself with great force through my navel. Today I am completely at peace.

I got a letter from her. The only person who writes me (who has become the great letter-writer of GP) is my mother. Usually it's not a letter but a card saying something like *Thinking of you*, with a twenty-dollar bill in it. But this letter is from my doctor lady friend.

> *Dear N. . . .*
>
> I recognized you when you came to get your face
> stitched up, but it would have been unprofessional of me

to do so openly. Please feel free to write to me from time to time, and try to keep the faith while you pay for your mistake. I will be praying for you.

Sincerely

S

Friends and neighbours, my teachers and classmates from prep school, my former professors, prison warders, Samora Machel, Agostinho Neto, Fidel Castro, Richard Hart, Walter Rodney, Millicent and Jackson, men from the private sector of Jamaica who are seated with my ex-comrades, are all assembled in the university chapel and I am standing at the altar, dressed in my flour-bag prison uniform with my friend the chain-smoking Canadian priest standing beside me. In what will become a sweet recurring dream, my doctor bride comes walking through the wide-open doors of the chapel as the music of the organ rolls like the waves of the sea.

Dream Lover

T HEY ARE SITTING on the beach out at Copacabana. It is one o'clock in the morning and the music from the disco is getting mellow now. These are the hours of rent-a-tile. Just the love songs now, lifting up and out over the St. Thomas beach with the big silver moon shimmying in the water, buffing the black sand. They can taste salt in their mouths.

"When are you going to let me?"

This is where she always pulls away from him and says something like, "Please don't pressure me, please."

"We could get married, you know. When you want to get married?"

She could just see herself going to tell her parents that she was going to get married at age nineteen to a twenty-two-year-old young man who was a teller in a bank and owned nothing besides an old beat-up VW bug.

"I love you, but I am not going to keep begging you."

"Hear 'Dream Lover' there. I want to dance."

"No, I'm going to swim."

And he strips down to his briefs and walks toward the water. Just before he dives in, he turns around and stands still, facing her. He is tall with broad shoulders and a body lean from playing soccer. He stands up under the floodlight of the full moon in just his white briefs and he says, "Look at what you are missing."

He jogs down to the water, dives into the night sea, and swims strongly away from her. She stands on the beach watching his head bobbing up and down. Sometimes he disappears from sight and she is afraid that he has drowned. She imagines herself running back up the beach to the paved thatched-roof area where the dancers are locked tight in their two-fifty-cents-in-a-dollar embraces. She imagines herself sounding the alarm – "HELP, HELP, COME QUICK, MY BOYFRIEND IS DROWNING!" – and everyone running down to the beach, and the police coming in late from the Bull Bay police station because the corporal had taken the one vehicle assigned to the station to carry home his girlfriend.

She imagines his body washed up cold on the sand, and her name in the newspapers, and for the rest of her life she would feel guilty knowing that he drowned because she wouldn't let him.

He comes out of the water and dries off with his big purple towel and changes back into his clothes. The towel serves as a cover for the ripped-up front seat of the VW. Sometimes he uses it as a blanket when his aunt with whom he boards in Rollington Town locks him out and he sleeps in the car. The old lady calls him Chlorodo, the name of a local laundry bleach because she says that he bleaches – that is, he stays out all night – so much. She is afraid of thieves, so she often puts the deadbolts on the doors before he gets home. Because of this, he keeps a change of clothes in the car at all times.

He wants to get married.

"Nobody could lock me out of my own house."

"Why don't you just rent your own place?"

"No. I want a wife and a house and a dog and some children."

The purple towel was what he had spread on the sand for them to lie on when they began to make out about half an hour ago. After his night swim he is in a better mood, but his hands and face are cold when he holds her and tells her: "Come, let's dance, but not to 'Dream Lover.' You want a dream lover but I want to be your real lover."

He begged her. He sent her padded and scented postcards that came in outsized envelopes and sent greetings to her on the radio requesting songs like Jackie Edwards singing "Tell Me Darling" and Keith & Enid's "Worried Over You." He bought her a pair of amethyst earrings and told her that amethysts meant sincerity. But mostly he asked her, begged her through the music. "Try me," he'd sing along with James Brown softly in her ear, and "Prisoner of Love" was his favourite song.

Diplomatic Relations, that is what her parents want her to study. A degree in Diplomatic Relations, leading to a job in the Foreign Service. But in the end he had travelled before her because he found somebody he did not have to beg; a plain-looking girl who worked in the bank with him. He got married just three months after he told her "I'm not going to beg you or pressure you anymore."

And he hadn't. He had just stopped calling and coming to see her.

When she heard that he was getting married and that he and his wife were going to go and live abroad, she had pretended that it didn't matter because, as she told everybody, it was she who did not want him. But she lost a lot of weight and she had to go to the doctor because she became so nervous and she couldn't sleep and the doctor had started her taking Valium.

Twenty-five years have passed. She is visiting Jamaica from London, England, where she has lived for fifteen years. She wants to go dancing to old hits, she wants to feel nineteen again. Her friends tell her, "My dear, you are late. Copa closed down long time and nobody in their right mind goes clubbing along the St. Thomas Road these days. Everybody fraid of gunman. If you really want to hear some oldies we'll take you up to New Kingston."

Even by the artificial moonlight in the nightclub she still recognizes him. All she can say as she feels her heart start to thump like the bass beat emanating from one of the man-sized sound boxes: "Ah, the prisoner of love himself." And he laughs and laughs and laughs and just folds her in his arms. "Did you find your dream lover?"

No. Much foreign travel, one marriage, one daughter, one divorce, and several near-marriages later, and no, she has not found her dream lover. She starts to ask him about his life, but he just says:

"Come, let me see if you can still dance."

He had taught her to dance the three-step.

"Just relax, don't do anything, just follow me."

He doesn't sing in her ear. He just holds on to her and closes his eyes tight and, just so, they three-step back into each other's lives.

Her friends could not believe it. Imagine meeting him again after twenty-five years.

It is only when the sweep of slow songs end and the dee-jay starts spinning some idiotic disco music that he brings her back to the table where her friends are sitting. He seats her, then goes off to the bar without asking her what she wants and comes back bearing a glass of ginger ale into which he pours some of his beer. He takes a sip from her glass before handing it to her. She starts to say, "You remembered," but he says "Let's go outside."

Standing outside in the car park of the nightclub, not too far from the security guard, she said, "We should be out at Copa."

"Yes, and by now I'd be swimming in the cold sea."

"How is your wife?"

"We divorced."

"Sorry it didn't work out. You really wanted to get married."

"You didn't want me."

"I wasn't ready."

"What about you?" She told him her story.

Then he tells her his news. He is getting married again.

As a matter of fact he is getting married, like King Yellow Man, in the morning.

"So what, no bachelor party?"

"At my age? You have to be joking. It's just a quiet little thing this time. I'm having a drink with a co-worker. Stay here, don't move, I'm going to get rid of him, tell your friends I'll drive you back to where you're staying."

"Oh god, look at you, you hardly look any older than, how old you were when me and you . . . nineteen? You don't look a day older than twenty. Jesus, I must be the saltest man who ever lived. Look when I find you again after all these years. I must have the worst luck in the world . . . You know, my ex-wife used to give me grief all the time about you. She always accused me of fantasizing about you. She said that I always stared at women in the street who looked short and sweet like you. If I didn't want to do something with her she would say, 'Yes, but if she asked you, you would do it, though.' She never once called your name in her mouth, she always said 'she.'"

And together they said, "And she is the cat's mother." And they stood there in the car park laughing under a big full moon, the asphalt paving gleaming like black sand.

In her room at the hotel before day, he told her, "Pretend that I am really the first one. That is who I wanted to be, your first and only one."

"I wish to God you had been."

"You belong to me?"

"I belong to you."

"If you had said yes on the beach at Copa, this is what I would have done to you."

"And then I'd have done this."

"No way. You didn't know anything about things like that in those days . . . Just tell me to stay."

"I can't tell you to stay."

"So what? I must let you go again?"

She and her dream lover and their hopeless timing. Their love that is always running counter to the rhythm. Timing off, like that of a hippie they had seen one night in Montego Bay, struggling against the rhythm of Toots and the Maytals stirring up "Dog War," never able to catch the beat at the right time. And they hold on to each other and rock in each other's arms like they would sometimes do after they had a quarrel and he used to say, "See how good I am at calming you down, girl? I'm going to make a very good father, you know."

"Are you going now?"

"Just tell me to stay and I won't go."

When he says that, she reaches over and switches on the lamp at the bedside.

"What do you mean by that?"

He does not answer, he just pulls hard and blows out a long streamer of smoke. In the past hour she had been aware of his presence every time she turned in her sleep. One time she turned over and he was sitting up in the bed looking down at her. She had reached up, touched his face, and said, "You really should try to get some rest."

Then she had turned over and fallen into a deep sleep. "I'm serious. If you tell me not to go, I'll just call now and say . . ."

She sat up in the bed and faced him.

"You must be mad! How could I ever tell you to do something like that?"

The sun will come up and she will tell him to go or not go. Or he will decide not to go or to go, but for now, in the before-day, they rock in each other's arms and the clock radio that has been on low all night will start to play Saturday oldies music.

~

Haul and pull up. That is what Jamaican deejays say when they want to begin a song over again. Sometimes they say, "Wheel and come again." This story needs to begin again, for it didn't really end like that.

Let's begin again then, but not from the top. Let's take it from where he gets tired of begging her and goes off and gets married to somebody else and she goes off to England and worked in the Diplomatic Service and got married, had a child, and gets divorced.

Her thirtieth birthday found her in Washington, D.C., at an official function where she struck up an instant friendship with a woman who worked at the United States Information Service. By the end of the function they were such fast friends that they headed off to have dinner together at a new West Indian restaurant run by a Jamaican woman and a Trinidadian man. The wife produced all the wonderful fusion cuisine while the husband did all the greeting and chatting up of customers. The partnership ended a year after the restaurant opened because the wife got tired of doing all the work.

"Are you sure my father didn't know your mother?"

"You are not going to believe this – but I have those shoes you are wearing in green."

"Oh listen, they are playing Third World. I saw them in concert in New York last year. Every time I hear 'Irie Ites,' I want to be in Negril."

"My dear, Ibo Cooper is a good friend."

"Oh really? You must introduce me sometime."

"What are you having? I'm having the 'rude-to-parents chicken' – breast of chicken sauteed in white rum sauce – and the 'likkle dis, likkle dat' rice."

"That is exactly what I was going to order."

"Oh look, look here. Surely we must try the 'puss prayers' – avocado salad to you."

They were both gigglers. The menu was good for ten full minutes of giggling.

"Cheers," said her new best friend from the USIS. "Happy thirtieth birthday . . . you know I turned thirty last year and you know what I found? I found out that everything goes deeper after age thirty. You just can't shrug things off so easily and you begin to have serious regrets."

Four hours after meeting this woman for the first time, she felt close enough to her to tell her all about her one true love.

"It's because of him why I love to dance, and I wish to God that I had said to hell with it and married him. He was a much better man any day than my joker of an ex-husband . . . I just know it would have worked. Him and me and that beat-up VW bug and the purple towel."

Over their "bowl a bwiling Blue Mountain cawfee" she told this woman whom she'd just met all about her one true love. The one she should have given herself to on the beach out at Copacabana under a full Jamaican moon. Her new best friend from USIS sat ever so quietly as she shared Oprah-style with her. Her new friend said nothing. She did not laugh about the VW and the purple towel. She never offered her advice like, "Why don't you look him up on the internet?" She just sat there silently with her mouth screwed enviously to one side; and suddenly she who had been planning for them to meet up again next month to go shopping announced that she had to go back to her hotel immediately because she was expecting a call.

And they both knew that that was the end of their instant friendship. Everything had changed when she mentioned her great love; that was one thing they did not have in common, and that was one thing the woman from the USIS would kill to have.

Having a great love gave her permission to choke up when she sat in a restaurant on a rainy day and heard Sarah Vaughn's crystalline voice promising to love "eternally" over the PA system. It made her grin broad encouragement at lovers who "sucked face," as her daughter would say, in public places in broad daylight. As one who had known a great love, she bought a voluminous black wool cape that she wore in winter with the hood up like the French Lieutenant's Woman even though she really was not tall enough for that look. Her great love gave her the right to give advice on matters to do with love with a kind of vehemence that some people found startling. "Take a chance," she'd insist to some undecided lover of her acquaintance. "Believe me, I know what I'm talking about when I tell you to take a chance or you will live to regret it."

And so when they did actually meet again in that night-club in New Kingston she willed herself to ignore the fact that his soccer-playing days were obviously way behind him. She willed herself to ignore the young girl he was with, whom he introduced as his co-worker. A girl who was wearing a skirt so short it was more like a wide belt. She barely heard when he said his wife was fine. That she was expecting their fourth child, which had come as a sweet "last lick" (his words) to them. His family? They lived in Miami, but he commuted. She heard when he said he was sure glad to see her after all this time and maybe they could go out for dinner the next night. When he said this, his co-worker nearly pitched over four tables as she kissed her teeth and flounced off.

"No," she said, dinner the next night did not look possible, for she had a diplomatic function to attend. "Too bad," he said, for he was going to Miami day after tomorrow because one of his children had a birthday. "So maybe next time," he said. She said, "Sure, maybe next time." And then, as she came face to face with the fact that maybe she was not really his one true love, she murmured softly to herself, "C'est la vie." And he, getting up to go in search of his co-worker, said to her, "What did you just say? You know I don't speak Spanish."

Miss Henny, Suliman Santer, and Me

Chetolah Park School was called shit-in-the park school by the good children of All Saints School. Miss Henny lived behind the teacher's cottage in a little one-roomed flat that stood by itself, separate from the big teacher's cottage. I never did find out how and why Miss Henny came to be living there.

At least once a week my mother would send me down to Chetolah Park School to take dinner in a covered dish wrapped in a linen napkin to Miss Henny (short for Henrietta) Marshall, who was related to my father. When I get to the gates of Chetolah Park School they are closed, and I see the watchman, Mr. Ryan, sitting on an old chair under a black mango tree. Mr. Ryan looks remarkably like the emperor of Ethiopia, Haile Selassie. A short, slight man with a pointed beard, he is always reading the *Gleaner* newspaper, or *Public Opinion*, or old copies of *The Watchman*. I don't think that he does much watching, though. He does not move to get up and unlock the big iron gate when he looks up and sees me standing there.

Not even after I tell him good morning and I say what I have come to think of as our password: "Keep cool, Mr. Ryan, keep cool." Mr. Ryan just looks as if he has never seen me before in his life. Now Mr. Ryan knows me – I come to see Miss Henny all the time. But he takes his watchman job very seriously.

"I come to see Miss Henny, sir."

"Miss Henny," he says, as if he has no idea who that could be and he has to mentally rummage through the crowded entries in his watchman's ledger. "Miss Henny, eh?"

Mr. Ryan likes to be important. Some Sunday afternoons I have seen him stepping in the front row of the Jones Town group of the United Negro Improvement Association, which marches up to Edelweiss Park, to attend rallies and meetings about their great leader, Mr. Marcus Garvey. I have seen Mr. Ryan holding a fringed velvet banner high over his head with the stout and serious countenance of Mr. Marcus Garvey woven into the pile of the velvet. Proclaimed in an arch over Mr. Garvey's head is "One God, One Aim, One Destiny." Mr. Ryan and the other members march to the sounds of big booming brass instruments, and their eyes all seem fixed in the direction of the Kingston Harbour, where they still believe that one day seven miles of Black Star liners will majestically dock in one of the world's seven natural harbours and take them all back to Africa from where the black people of Jamaica were stolen.

This same Mr. Ryan, who is going on as if he has never seen me before in his life, has spoken to me about Mr. Garvey. One day he had looked up and seen me returning from taking Miss Henny's dinner to her and said:

"Little miss, do you know about Mr. Marcus Garvey?"

I said yes I had heard his name, and that I had read something in the *Gleaner* that said he was a rascal, a criminal, and a troublemaker.

And Mr. Ryan told me that that was not true, that Mr. Garvey was a great, great man who believed in the dignity of black people, who said that black people were a mighty race. That they should learn to think for themselves, to govern themselves, and to have their own businesses. He told me that Jamaican people did not know this, but that the United Negro Improvement Association was once one of the largest organizations in the world. He said that Mr. Garvey was one of the greatest leaders in the world, and because of this they had lied and falsely imprisoned him. Mr. Ryan said that some Jamaican black people had sold Marcus Garvey for food.

"Sell him for rice and peas, for rice and peas," he had said, bitterly shaking his head from side to side. "For rice and peas."

"Some people just too craven," I had said to Mr. Ryan. Mr. Ryan had looked really sad at that moment, his light-brown eyes brimming with tears. Then he had just started to chant to himself:

> *Let no trouble worry you*
> *Keep cool, keep cool*
> *Don't get hot like some folks do*
> *Keep cool, keep cool*

"Mr. Garvey write that song, you know, little miss," he had told me as I stepped past him to go home. I left him sitting under the mango tree with his eyes shut tight, chanting to himself:

> *Throw your troubles far away*
> *Smile a little every day*
> *And the sun will start to shine*
> *Making life so true and fine*
> *Do not let a little care*
> *Fill your life with grief and fear*
> *Just be calm, be brave and true*
> *Keep your head and you'll get through*
> *Keep cool, keep cool.*

Thereafter, every time I saw Mr. Ryan I would say, "Keep cool, Mr. Ryan, keep cool."

I thought that after that he would surely know me when I came to the gate. After a while he suddenly raised a forefinger, tapped his forehead, and said:

"Ah, Miss Henny. You know, I think that I see her sitting under the tamarind tree taking some cool breeze this morning."

Only then does he open the gate and allow me to go through.

Miss Henny is sitting up in bed, dressed in a pink flannel nightgown. When I tell her that Mr. Ryan says he saw her sitting under the tamarind tree, she says:

"Mr. Ryan saw me? Me, Henrietta Justina Marshall, outside under the tamarind tree? That man's mind has been wandering since Marcus Garvey pass away, and he must be seeing duppy now, because I have not put my foot outside even once today."

"What is wrong with you, Miss Henny," I ask as I put the covered dish on her dining table. Before she answers me she says, "Thank God and thank your mother." She always says that, in that order. She told me that you should always thank God first. No matter who had given you a gift, it was God who had given it to them to give to you.

Then she says:

"No definite complaint, my child. It is just that when you are old as me you don't feel as good as when you are young and, seeing as how I do not have chick nor child to answer to, I could stay in bed ten days straight if I want to."

Miss Henny has travelled all over the world. Her husband, Charles, was in the West India Regiment and she went with him after they got married to Sierra Leone in Africa. She told me many stories about Africa. She always says, "Let me give you a story," as if was a present she was giving. Miss Henny would give me a story for every problem I brought to her. My absolute favourite story had to do with Major Madden and Suliman Santer.

She said that her husband had gone with E Company Regiment up to the Gambia on the west coast of Africa to call upon Chief Suliman Santer to come to a palaver. I guess the British did not like how Suliman was behaving so they felt that a palaver was in order.

"Yes," said Miss Henny, "a palaver is what they called a meeting, so when you hear Jamaican people talking about a palaver, it does not just mean susu or gossip. The real African meaning is a meeting."

Miss Henny then enters into the telling of the story, of how the regiment travelled by boat to Suliman's fort, which he had built out of mud.

"Mud, the living mud. My husband, Charles, said you should have seen the helluva fort that this African built out of mud. He said that when the boats with the soldiers reached to a creek, they had to pass through a deep swamp and then walk through yards upon yards of deep mud before they reach to Suliman's fort with some high, high, towers made out of living mud."

The leader of the regiment, one Major Madden, called out to Suliman:

"Suliman Santer, I command you this day to attend a palaver with the representatives of her majesty Queen Victoria."

By this time Miss Henny was standing up as straight as her bandy legs would allow her, with her arms held stiffly by her side in imitation of a military stance, as she called upon hard-ears Suliman Santer to come out and palaver with the representatives of Her Majesty. "Well, ma'am, Suliman kiss him teeth, *cheeups*, and did not even fennay pon Major Madden, and then proceed to fire some big gun, *boom boom* on Her Majesty's soldiers."

At this point, Miss Henny demonstrates how Suliman fired the big gun. She stoops slightly, squinches up her eyes as she stretches one arm forward to serve as the muzzle of the gun, and makes a pulling action under her elbow with the thumb and forefinger of her other hand to fire the trigger of the rifle.

"Then one brave Jamaican soldier see Suliman aiming a gun through one of the loopholes in his mud fort straight at Major Madden and call out, 'Look out, sir,' and throw himself between Major Madden and the bullet."

At this point Miss Henny throws herself sideways and lands on her bed. "The bullet went right into that poor man's lungs. My husband, Charley, say that with all the man had a bullet in him, he was so valiant that when they come with a hammock to carry him back to the boat, he refused the hammock and made them give it to the Englishman who was wounded too. That brave Jamaican man walk all the way back to the boat bleeding from the bullet in his lungs.

"Queen Victoria gave the man a medal," said Miss Henny, sitting up in her bed. "Charles, my husband, never got any medal, for he was a man who loved his life too much to go and risk it for Major Madden. After all, Major Madden was no friend to Charles. No sir, you wouldn't find my husband risking him good good life just so. Anyway, when Queen Victoria gave the man the medal, you know what she said? She said that the man was never to be tried by court martial no matter what bad thing he should do. Charles said that was ungracious of Queen Victoria. It was as if she was expecting the man to go and do something bad notwithstanding all the good the man had done. So the moral of that story is: if Queen Victoria herself don't know how to tell a proper thanks, what says the ordinary Jamaican people?"

Miss Henny had visited the United States of America.

She said that she once went into a store in New York City and the shopkeeper said to her, "Huloo, darky." Years later, when I went to New York for the first time I half expected all the shopkeepers in the city to greet me with "Huloo, darky" but of course they didn't, and I guess I never really expected them to. But I always remembered how they greeted Miss Henny.

There are many photographs of Miss Henny and her husband on the mahogany bureau in her room. It is a beautiful mahogany bureau with an oval mirror set on hinges so that it can be tilted up or down, and the pulls on the drawers are made from some pinkish marblelike stones, which dangle like the drop earrings of a gorgeous woman. The bureau is right next to the high iron-frame bed. Over in one corner of the room there is a small table with two chairs, and at the foot of the bed is my favourite thing in the room, Miss Henny's big brass trunk. She told me it was called a steamer trunk, and it is covered with labels with the names of various ships on which she has sailed.

Carefully folded in tissue paper in the trunk is her wedding dress and veil. She says she travelled with them to every place that she went. One day she opened the trunk, which smelled of khus khus grass and mothballs, and showed them to me. When she placed the pearl-studded coronet with the mist of yellowing net on her head, she looked like a very old angel.

Miss Henny's skin is the exact colour of Mackintosh's toffee. It is toffee that comes in a roll from England, and is also called Toff-O-Luxe. She has a large nose like most of my father's people, and most of her teeth have gone so her lips looked wrinkled up, kind of like my mother gathered them up with the presser-foot of her sewing machine. But she has the prettiest dark eyes that flash and grow bright when she laughs and, although she is old, her face is not really wrinkled, it just looks more like an overripe mango.

She has very thin hair through which you can see her pink scalp. When her fine plaits become undone, her sparse white hair blows about her head until she catches it under a hairnet. Miss Henny has trouble with her hip bones so she rocks from side to side when she walks. I always think of her in connection with the sea. Her profile looks like the figure-head on the prow of a ship, and she walks with a sailor's rolling gait, catching her floating hair in a net.

I tell Miss Henny all of my little problems. Like the time Miss Stirling, the teacher at All Saints School, pulled me out of the choir before the whole school and announced that I had no business in the choir because I could not sing. "This little girl," she said, pulling me by the sleeve of my white middy blouse, "this little girl cannot sing at all." She plucked me from the lineup of singers where I had been joyfully adding my voice to "Flow Gently, Sweet Afton," and banished me to the percussion band where I was assigned a triangle, the stupidest and most babyish of all instruments. I had been so humiliated that instead of going home after school I had gone down to Miss Henny. When I told her what had happened she said, "That is nonsense. Everybody can sing."

And that is how she and I came to begin singing together there in her little room behind the teacher's cottage of Chetolah Park School. In between our singing, she would "give" me all kinds of stories and remedies, like which bush could be used to cure what complaint. Miss Mirry, our helper, knew all that stuff too, but she would never tell me anything because she really just hated me. But that's another story.

Miss Henny told me these things:

"If you have a toothache, boil some gungoo peas leaves and soak your mouth in the water. If you have a boil, quail a pepper leaf over the fire, put it on the boil, and it will draw up all the inflammation and break it open, saving you the pain of cutting it open. A pregnant woman must drink thyme tea to make her womb contract, and she must eat plenty plenty okra so that the baby can slide out smooth smooth."

If my mother ever knew that Miss Henny was discussing such big woman matters with me in her little room behind the Chetolah Park School she would have been horrified. My mother would never ever have discussed anything to do with pregnancy with me when I was aged ten as I was then, not in one million years.

"If you hear those lions roar outside the army camp at night, your heart quake. Sometimes elephants go stark staring mad and trample down a whole village, especially when they suffer from toothache."

One night when I couldn't sleep and I lay there in the bed that I shared with my sister, it occurred to me that if only those elephants could have soaked their mouths with that gungoo peas infusion, many villages in Africa might have been spared. When I asked Miss Henny if I could try on her bridal veil, she said no, it would bring down bad luck on me if I did that. She also advised me never to take the last piece of cake, because I would end up as an old maid.

Miss Henny taught me the words to "(There'll Be Bluebirds Over) The White Cliffs of Dover." She told me that they used to sing that song in England when they were looking forward to the ending of the war, and she would cry when she sang that song because she said that she and her husband would sing that song whenever they were parting from each other, and now that he was dead that song always made her cry. Her voice would shake up the words then, and she would close her pretty dark eyes.

Sometimes she would pause in the middle of that song and ask me to pass the photograph of her husband in his uniform from the bureau. I would bring her the heavy silver-framed photograph of a man standing straight with his arms by his sides. The photograph was now brownish yellow and the man wore three-quarter-length trousers with two thin stripes running down the front seams. He had on what looked like white boots and he wore a blouse-looking shirt with full sleeves, a bolero vest over it, and a headwrap like a poco-mania shepherd. Everything in the photograph was fading. It was as if Miss Henny's husband, Charles, was backing away from the open field into the tent in the background.

Miss Henny would take the photograph and clasp it to her bosom, and then she would hold it out in front of her and sing to it. "Yes, Charley," she would sing in her trembling, shaken-up voice, "there will be bluebirds over the white cliffs of Dover, tomorrow just you wait and see." And then she would gaze earnestly at the photograph, with tears streaming down her face. Then she would rest it tenderly on her bosom, and we would always get quiet after that. Maybe one of us would hum a snatch of one of the songs we had been singing, but usually we stopped singing after Miss Henny had serenaded her husband's photograph.

In our post-blue-birds-over-the-white-cliffs silence, we would look through the window of the little room. We could see Mr. Ryan still sitting under the mango tree reading his old newspapers. Once I asked her if we could sing "Flow Gently, Sweet Afton," for that is what I had been singing when Miss Stirling threw me out of the choir. But before we sang it I wanted to ask her a question. "Miss Henny, what is a 'brae'? You know the song says 'Flow gently, sweet Afton, among thy green braes'?"

"Hmmn. 'Flow gently, sweet Afton, among thy green braes,'" sings Miss Henny to herself, going over the words. "Well, it cannot be like a donkey's bray because the song says this bray is green. And the song says 'My Mary is asleep by thy murmuring stream,' so we know that the Afton is a murmuring stream. So if you are telling the Afton to flow among the green brays, then a brae must be like a field or some place that a river flows through." Years later I found out that a brae is a hill, but Miss Henny had given me my first lesson in understanding how to read a poem, how to get to the sense of it.

So we sang "Flow Gently, Sweet Afton," and then Miss Henny asked me to go to the shop and buy her a loaf of HTB hard-dough bread. When I came back she gave me two big shiny copper willy pennies as a gift because she said a person should not just be receiving all the time. She explained to me once that they were called willy pennies because the profile of the big-headed man on the coins was that of Prince William, who Jamaican people referred to in their familiar way as Willy.

I went home past Mr. Ryan, who by now was fast asleep in his chair, leaving me to open and close the gate myself. When I got home I told my mother about Miss Henny staying in bed because she "had neither chick nor child to answer to."

Eventually Miss Henny's relatives decided that she could not live by herself any more, so they came and took her, her iron bed, her table and chairs, and her steamer trunk faraway to the country.

O my friend, Miss Henny, I know that you are sitting up in your bed somewhere in the sky. I want to tell you that some days I feel like Suliman Santer; not in the least bit inclined to palaver with the Major Maddens of this world, the interfering legions who want to invade my fortress made of living mud. But neither do I want to shoot them. I just want to give because I have received and flow gently like the sweet Afton among green braes and Blue Mountains, before I shake up the words again.

Mi Amiga Gran

~

AT 11:00 P.M. I finish studying for my History test. Ask me anything, anything at all about the reign of Henry the Eighth or any other Tudor and I can tell you. You know which one of them died from a surfeit of lampreys and ale? Ask me and I tell you. I'm going to koof that test tomorrow. Sleep time now, Anna. I haul my red blanket up under my chin, but when I do that, what do I see but my big toe? I have to bend my knees for my toe to take cover. Six months ago when I came here, this blanket covered my body from head to foot. Jeezam! As you say "body," I just remember that the white shorts and T-shirt that must cover mine in gym class tomorrow are in a funky grey ball at the bottom of the clothes cupboard.

Options, Anna. Examine your options. That is what Miss Patsy Patterson, my English teacher, would say. My options are to a) jump up now and take the dirty gym clothes into the bathroom, give them a lick and a promise with the Palmolive soap, hang them over the shower curtain rod, and try to get up early tomorrow morning and dry them with the iron, which means I am bound to scorch them; b) I could write an excuse to Miss Mcintosh, the gym teacher, and sign it myself. *Dear Miss Mcintosh, Please excuse Anna from gym class as she is unwell. Sincerely, Mrs. I. Lampheart (Guardian).*

Unwell. I learned that word from my grandmother. FYI it means a lot more than just not feeling well. PE teachers are supposed to know what *unwell* really means; it means they are supposed to excuse you from playing netball and doing jumping jacks and other sweaty exercises if you are unwell. I decided to go with the unwell letter, as I felt myself slipping deeper into sleep even though Tiffany Lampheart keeps her radio on twenty-four seven.

"Just get up and go on to school."

That was my tender morning greeting from Mrs. L, who is not happy with me these days because my boarding money is late. She is just barely giving me two meals a day since last week, and yesterday I heard her daughter, Tiffany, the ten-watt bulb, talking on the phone about "people whose parents leave them to freeload in other people's houses." All because the U.S. dollars that my mother sends for my board and lodging every month have not come yet. I accidentally turned over her bottle of shampoo in the bathroom after I heard her say that.

I hope the eagle lands soon, for I spend off all my last month's pocket money. My mother boarded me here when she went to the States. I would never be here if my Grandma Love had not "gone to a silent home," as she same one would say. Up till now, two years later, I can't believe how she just gone and leave me. Me, her *pasero*, her *amiga. Ai caramba.* If Grandma Love didn't go into the hospital with pneumonia and not come out, I wouldn't have to be living here with the Lamphearts, who really don't, in their heart, check for people who look like me. But I guess if I cover myself with the strong dollars that my mother sends, I look fine to them. My mother left for New York in a hurry; she found this place for me by looking in the newspaper in an advertisement that said, "Boarding for female student available in spacious upper St. Andrew home, U.S. dollars preferred." This is how I come to be sharing a pink room decorated with one hundred pink and silver unicorns with T. Lampheart.

Grandma Love use to live in Panama and Cuba when she was young, so she would mix up English and Spanish, I guess you could call it Spanglish. She used to say, "Ai, ai, ai. Mi miss mi Silver City, Colon." She said that even though Panama used to have a system like apartheid, it was based on gold and silver. Honest to God! Silver shops were for black people and gold shops for white people. That is before Jamaicans went there and you know how we stay, we the people from Jamdown insisted on shopping in the gold shops and brukking fight for the right so to do, causing the silver and gold system to vanish away. Still, she said she would always miss Colon.

I think that her love for Panama had to do with her old boyfriend, a short little hombre in a panama hat named Rodrigo whose yellow photograph and even yellower letters Grandma was always reading and going, "Hee hee heeee, *mi amor*, you too rude. What a man rude!"

A singer name Celia Cruz was like Whitney Houston to Grandma. Sometimes she would tune in to the Cuban radio station and shake up herself to the music, "*Ai, caramba, chica,* *you should see me when I danza the samba and the meringue,*" and she would haul me up to dance with her. "*Caramba chica,* *mi pasero.*" Gran used to tell some corny jokes about what happened to people who work hard for the money in Cuba and Panama and how con men used to prey on them.

A corny but nice story from Grandma Love:

"One time, you know, Miss Anna, this man was walking down King Street, well dressed in him grey serge suit and a black felt hat. Him had a big gold watch with a long chain. Them time there them used to have a song you know that say:

> *One, two, three, four, Colon man a come,*
> *One, two, three, four, Colon man a come*
> *With him brass chain a lick him belly,*
> *bam, bam, bam.*
> *Me ask him fi the time and him look up a the sun*
> *Ask him fi the time and him look up a the sun*
> *Still him brass chain a lick him belly, bam, bam, bam.*

"Well, missus, this Kingston ginnal step up to him and say, 'Hey, a me and you a twoa,' and him hold up two finger to show say that him and the man was close friend. Well, mi love, the man just hold up three finger and say, 'Yes? And you and me and the gun in my pocket a threeya.'"

I know that this sounds bad, but I miss my grandmother way more than I miss my mother. "The oldest living teenager in captivity," as a certain deejay on the radio would say. My mother who fly gone to New York after her boyfriend, Max, who style himself as an "entertainer." My mother deals strictly with entertainers. My father was one. He jumped ship before I was born. All I have from my father is a few forty-five records, none of which ever hit a hit parade. I mean, what kind of butto would cut a record called "Lick-and-Run Man?" Don't that should have pripped my mother that the man was not looking for a lasting relationship? Maybe "the oldest teenager" is probably not working and that is why my boarding money is late. O God, I hope she is all right.

Well, crowdapeople, here is Anna at lunchtime, except that Anna has no lunch. At school we have a breakfast feeding program for poor girls, you come early and they give you some lumpy cornmeal porridge and a slice of day-old bread that one of the old girls who owns a bakery contributes to the program. Fortunately Mrs. Lampheart already allowed me to have some cornmeal porridge this morning, so no worries. But if the money does not come from my mother soon, what is going to happen to me? I might have to join the poor girl's breakfast program, and soon Mrs. Lampheart will throw me out into the street so I will have to go and live at Maxfield Park Children's Home.

Anna Imagines Life at Maxfield Park

It is Christmas at the Maxfield Park Children's Home and a well-dressed lady arrives in a new chauffeur-driven Benz. She steps out and heads toward the hall where the children are assembled. The chauffeur follows behind her bearing a box of modest size containing gifts.

"Are the photographers from the newspaper here yet?" asks the lady.

"No," says the matron of the home, who has arranged the children in neat rows, the smallest at the front and the older ones who will soon be turned out onto the street in the back row.

"Well, I will not be distributing these gifts till the press shows up."

The children look at the box like dogs at a big beef bone.

The chauffeur stands guard over the box as if contains all the jewellery in Swiss stores. The well-dressed woman returns to her car to wait on the newspaper photographer. Some of the children start to cry.

"The lady give you any present to put down?" asks one of the attendants, clamping her hand over the mouth of one little girl who cries louder than all the other children.

The newspaper photographer arrives. The lady powders her face, puts on more red lipstick, and comes back and hands out the gifts, looking all the time straight at the camera. There are not enough toys to go around, so she opens a box of crayons and hands one single crayon to each child who did not receive a toy. By the time she gets to the last child who was crying louder than the rest, all she has left is a white crayon. The well-dressed lady hands the white crayon to the child who wails even louder than before.

The end

I am too old to live at Maxfield Park Children's Home, so I will have to leave school and go and get a job (but where, doing what?) or I will end up living on the street and become involved with one of the big-belly, nasty, old youth, whiteshoes man who cruise bus stops in their criss cars and pick up licky-licky school girls. I will become a worthless, bruk-down skettel when I begin to live what Grandma Love called "kayliss life." At this stage I am forced to put my imagination in check.

By now you know about my imagination. When I was small, some people said things like, "You must stop her from tell lie," but Gran said "Leave her, the child have imagination." I want to become a writer. I'm going to graduate from high school next year, and I'm either going to go to UWI or to the States to join my mother and Max — that is, if Max is still on the scene. My friend Marcia is a serious *amiga*, she sees me sitting under the divi-divi tree and just comes over and hands me a paper bag with a patty and a box juice. Last week she was giving me her sandwiches, saying how she was on a diet, or paying me back for some debt I don't know anything about.

"Yes, Anna, man. You don't remember that you pay my fare at Carib last month?"

"You know, Marcia, you are my *pasero*."

"And you are *mi amiga*."

The money from my mother did not come when I got home that evening, but I did get another letter. It was from my grandmother's younger brother, who was as old as Methuselah and who lived in Bog Walk. His name was Berrisford Donnally.

I rip open the envelope and two green-and-black hundred dollar bills flutter out like doctor birds. His handwriting looked like a wrought-iron gate.

> *Dear Anna,*
>
> How keeping, I hope these few words find you in the best of health. I dream my sister last week and she says that I am to send something for you. This is all I have for now. When my pension from England arrives at month end I will send something more. Be a good girl, put your head to your book, and stay sweet.
>
> *Yours sincerely,*
> *Uncle Berris*

My *pasero*, my gran working from her grave to help me out. I start to dance a rhumba merengue skank, and just then Mrs. Lamps pushes the door.

"Anna, what the hell is the matter with you and your mother? I thought she was a responsible person, I cannot continue to board you if she does not live up to her obligations. Had I known that this was going to happen I would never have agreed blablablabla." This is one woman who can never just talk when she can give you a homily on the sins of the tavern (we are doing Chaucer in English class). She is also one of the most sharkish people in the world when it comes to money. The woman even looks like a shark, with her helluva nose and her gully mouth with a dangerous-looking set of teeth. The only time she ever says a kind word to me is when my mother sends her a bundle of U.S. dollars.

I suspect that she steams open any letters that come to me, because her damn nose is not big for nothing. I figure that she already checked out Uncle Berris's letter so I hand her one hundred-dollar bill, but she just stares at it and keeps holding out her hand. I was hoping to keep one to buy some "feminine products," as Marcia and me call it, but shark Lampheart is not budging, so I hand her the second bill. Her fin-fist closes around the two hundred dollars and she walks out of the room . . . Nengy nengy nengy. "I can barely feed my own child much more to go and take up a complete stranger's burden" – Nengy nengy nengy – "and this two hundred Jamaican dollars is nothing." Nengy nengy.

You know, technically I don't owe Mrs. Lampheart any money because my mother paid her a month's damage deposit in advance when I moved here. As far as I know I have not done any damage to their place. But since this woman is so hard as to deprive me of one hundred dollars to buy sanitary pads, I use some from the giant-sized box that her daughter stores in the pink bathroom that the two of us are supposed to share. The next day when I go to take some more, the box is nowhere in sight. I have to do a thing with toilet paper until I go to school and Marcia, *mi amiga*, helps me out.

Although I personally think I am just fine, some people might say I am not a pretty girl. At least not the way that, say, Tiffany Lampheart, who is a bona fide browning, is pretty. In the room where she and her mother allow me to kotch, most of the space is taken up with her standing hair dryer, her mani/pedi equipment, her wardrobe rammed with clothes, and her various bottles of creams and lotions. She sets her hair on about one hundred pink rollers every night, so she sleeps on a special satin pillowcase. My hair is natural and I don't wear makeup, I like myself that way. The first week that I came here I overheard Tiffany chatting me with one of her friends: "Oh, you know our new boarder, Mrs. Kunta Kinte." It's all right, because Marcia and I started calling Tiffany "Pretty Dunce." Now everybody at school calls her that. Although we sleep in the same room and go to the same school, Tiffany Lampheart and me just don't mel!

Gran used to work for a lady in Panama who was a cosmetologist. According to her, the lady was really "a scientist" who conducted "experiments." Gran learned to make her own hair oil from a formula invented by the lady, Senora Castilla. I still have about six bottles of Gran's hair oil left. She used to cook it up in a big old iron pot, using castor oil and coconut oil and some other oil. She would put in aloes and perfume and other things – to tell the truth I'm not sure what she put in it – to make this "pomade" as she called it, which smells like jasmine and really makes your hair shine. To me, it always looked like a burn that collected water when she put a big blob of it on the back of her hand. She used to put a heavy black curling iron on the gas stove until it was smoking hot, then she would stand up before the mirror, part her hair into four, plaster some of the oil from the blob on her hand on to her scalp, and then run the hot comb through her hair and fry it straight.

"Gran, Gran, mine you burn off your ears." The smoke and fry hair smell was dread! I never allowed her to press my hair, no way, so she would cane row it for me and call me her beautiful African princess. So what if the Pretty Dunce call me Mrs. Kunta Kinte? I would check that guy who played Kunta Kinte in *Roots* any day.

The weekend is the worst. At least during the week I can go to school and come in late. On Friday I had to wear a dirty uniform, because the helper has been told not to wash any clothes at all for me. I spend most of the day keeping my arms close to my side because I'm sure I have green arm. I spend most of Saturday in the Tom Redcam Library just to get away from feeling like the leper in the Lampheart household. I wrote to my mother telling her about my situation and last night I asked Mrs. Lamps if I could call her. The phone is another problem. There is a wooden box beside it and she insists that anybody besides herself and her family have to pay ten dollars for a phone call. So, if, for example, I need to call Marcia because I forgot my homework, I have to fork out ten dollars. I finally convince her to make me call my mother collect. She places the call herself, but my mother's number rings and rings without an answer. Shark Lampheart slams down the receiver and looks at me like I'm an alien. She hawks and says something about how she will never make a mistake like this again. I try to watch TV to take my mind off my troubles and she comes and turns it off, saying, "Nobody is helping me to pay my electricity bill."

I have one friend around here. I didn't grow up in this area and I only moved here at the beginning of this term, so I don't really know anybody on the street except Johnny, who lives in the house at the corner. He goes to KC and we started talking because we take the same African Taxi, as we call the minibus. He is the closest thing I have to a boyfriend. I don't have to tell you that that is another thing Mrs. Lampheart has against me. She suspects that all young people are busily fornicating. All young people except of course her daughter, Tiffany, whose ambition is to win every beauty and modelling contest in Jamaica by any means necessary.

Speaking of fornication. There was a stinking scandal at our school last year when this man decided to check on his daughter in the middle of the school day and found that she was not in school. Well, seeing as how he had dropped her off at the school gate that morning, her father nearly had a heart attack when the school told him that they had not seen the girl for at least two months. Check this. Every morning she would dress in her uniform, take up her school bag, and have her parents drop her at the school gate. As soon as they left, she would peel off up to Half Way Tree and catch a taxi round to her boyfriend's apartment. Her boyfriend, who drives a black-on-black Bimmer, has three baby mothers, and is "self-employed." Miss Lady would spend the day flexing with him and then come back in time to stand up at the school gate for Mummy or Daddy to pick her up after school. She manage to do this for two months before her dolly house mash up.

I walk down to the corner and check Johnny. His mother kindly offers me some of their stew peas dinner. His mother is a sweet woman, she can't stand Mrs. Lampheart. Johnny said something like what was happening to me happened to a boy at Kingston College. His parents stopped sending his boarding money and the people he was boarding with turned him out. Johnny said that the guy started to live at the school, sleeping in the gym at nights on one of the exercise pallets. The watchman and his wife allowed him to wash his uniform and iron it once a week at their little house behind the school. Sometimes they gave him some food. It was only when the poor youth got flu and was too sick to get up one Monday morning that a teacher discovered him. It was the English teacher who said when he saw the boy lying there, "Ho, sleeper, awaken!"

Luckily the Old Boys' Association came together and helped to sponsor him till he took his exams. But after that everybody called the poor guy Ho, Sleeper. Lord, Johnny, suppose that happen to me? Suppose I have to start living at school? But our watchman wouldn't play that. He would inform on me right away. O God, Johnny, then I will have to go and live at Maxfield Park! Johnny is a practical person — he reminds me that I am too old for Maxfield Park. He is right. He tells me that I should try to be cool, that I must hear from my mother soon. "She must call," he kept saying. "You must hear from her."

He lends me fifty dollars that he borrows from his sister who is working. I promise that I will pay her back as soon as my money comes. So that is how I get lunch money for the next few days. When I get back to Mrs. Lampheart's house she has put the inside bolt on the front door although it's only 9:00 p.m. I knock quietly at first, then I have to knock really loud before she comes and lets me in, saying, "Why you breaking down my door? You paying the mortgage on my house?" Then she says, "This damn foolishness soon come to an end. After all, I'm not running a charitable institution." My boarding money is now nearly a month overdue.

On Sunday when it is time for dinner, Mrs. Lampheart calls everybody but me to the table. I decide to go and sit out in the backyard. I sit down in the backyard on a little rickety stool the helper uses because she is not allowed to sit in any of the chairs in the house. There is nothing I can do. Sometimes when Gran had some problem or the other she would reach a point when she would say, "I learn what I was to learn from this, there is nothing more I can do and I'm not saying one word more about this. Peace, be still." And after that you would never hear her say another word about whatever it was. I can smell the Sunday-dinner fried plantain. I just remember something about Gran and plaintain.

Three years ago I was crushing on this guy who was the drummer in the band that Max, my mother's boyfriend, was trying to put together. The boy was what Marcia call "eye candy." He must have been at least twenty-three with some cute dreads. I was wearing my tightest jeans every time the band practise at the house, and believe me the drummy was sending me some sexy vibes. Well, Gran read up the play, because one day she came home from the market with some big fit-looking ripe plantains and called me into the kitchen. "Miss Anna, come look here." She proceed to chop one of the plaintains in two. "Although the outside look ripe, inside the flesh young and stainy, force ripe! This plantain spoil because it force ripe." I got the message.

Anna, I say to myself, try not to think about the rice and peas and roast beef and fried plantains that Mrs. Lampheart and her family are devouring inside.

I sit on the helper's stool in the backyard and imagine

how I will have to drop out of school and become a domestic helper. I will have to wash other people's frowsy clothes, clean their untidy houses, scrub out their dirty bathrooms, and have them suspect me of thiefing anything they can't find. I could really get off on imagining myself in this situation. But then I think, So what? Gran used to do domestic work in Panama, before she studied her "cosmetology." If it comes to that, that I have to do domestic work to survive, I can do it. As a matter of fact, I intend to wash my own clothes from now on because I don't want anybody to handle me like Lampheart ever again. And if and when my pocket money comes I'm going to save some of it and not just spend it "like a sailor," as Gran used to say. And if the worst come to the worst and I don't hear from my mother this week, I will drop out of school and go and kotch with old Uncle Berris in Bog Walk and try to finish school down there. This is what I learned from this situation. Peace, be still, you hear, Gran. Peace, be still, *mi amiga*, Gran. Peace, be still, *mi* Gran. Peace, be still. I say things like that till a settled feeling comes over me. Then I go inside and hold a Sunday afternoon nap instead of a Sunday dinner. I can barely get into my bed as Pretty Dunce has now spread out her things all over the room. I have to step over at least five pairs of her womb-twister high heels to get to bed.

I wake up to hear Mrs. Lampheart calling, "Anna, Anna, someone is here to see you." I go out to the living room where I see a tall blond man with a bandana round his forehead. The man hair well braid and bead off, the man ears have in more earrings than Pretty Dunce.

"Irie. You're Anna, right? Well, the I mother asked the I to bring this for the I. Sorry it's so late. But, as you yardies say, no problem, mon."

Earring man hands me a parcel and a thick envelope.

"The I is on the way to the airport, so 'One love.'"

"Thank you, thank you very much," I say to him. I am so happy to see the envelope and the parcel that, believe me, I want to kiss earring man who reeks of Coconut Joe suntan oil and colly weed. I almost kiss him, that is how happy I am as I take my things from him. I swear that sand drops off the envelope when I tear it open. Maybe earring man, who looks like an old pirate, buried my treasure to keep it safe while he was down there in Negril. In the envelope there are two sets of American dollars. I take the stack with Mrs. Lampheart's name clipped to it and hand it to her. Then I go into the back-yard to read my mother's letter.

Dear Anna,

Can't stop now, I'm sending this (two months' boarding) with one of Max's friends so it will reach to you fast. (Ha ha.) I will be out of touch for the next six weeks as Max and band have some gigs across the States and I'm travelling with them as manager. Study hard, hope you like the new outfit.

Love,

Moms

Instead of delivering the letter and the parcel before he went to the North Coast, Henry Morgan decided to head straight to Negril, for sin, sun, and fun, and it is only now that he is on his way back to New York, nearly a month later that he is delivering my things.

I just sit on the helper's stool and rock back and forth with relief.

Hear me, the evil Mrs. Lampheart is nowhere in sight now that she is in possession of U.S. dollars.

"Anna, Anna dear, would you like some supper?"

I'm a different Anna now that I have my spending money. "No, thank you, Mrs. Lampheart." I go inside, shower, wash my hair, shine it up with some of Gran's pomade, and put on the new jeans and T-shirt that came in the parcel. Whoa! Me in the latest California-style jeans make the Pretty Dunce — who would commit murder/suicide to have these legs — to swell up like a bullfrog. Good. I walk down to the corner, pay back my boy Johnny his sister's money, and ask him if I can call Marcia on his phone.

Then I say to him, "*Mi amigo,* how aboutta you and me (holding up two fingers) catcha African Taxi up to Sovereign Plaza and go eata lotta junk food. My treat (holding up three fingers) with Marcia who say she will meeta us at the food court?" And because Johnny, or "Juanny" as I call him some-times, knows all about Gran, my guardian angel, he says, "*Si, chica. Si.*"

I Come Through

THE OTHER NIGHT out at Inn on the Ocean when I finished singing, the place was just quiet, quiet. All you could hear was the waves slapping against the concrete wall; it was like everybody in the place stopped breathing when I sing:

> I thought I'd touched bottom.
> I was still sinking in miry clay.
> The dark voice called "You,
> I want you for my woman
> you are going to be mine today."
> That's when I recall the promise.
> that his reign was only for a time,
> I shout, "get thee behind me, Satan
> no no not me, no, not this time."
> And that's when I rise up like new
> I come over, I give thanks, I come through.

It took a little while before the applause started, then it went on like it would never stop, wave after wave rolling up to the bandstand, sound waves washing my feet. Some of the women and the barmaid were crying; and a young girl in a blue dress, who was sitting at a table with some people in this music business, some people that I personally have no use for, some people who mix up in some terrible things, jumps up as if she catch the spirit and shout out:

"You sing for all of us, for all of us."

At least an hour and a half passed before my manager knocked at the door of my hotel room. The girl in the blue dress was with him. My new manager, who is a very considerate young man, knows by now that right after I finish a performance I'm hungry enough to eat half a cow although I don't eat red meat. The other thing he knows is that when the applause starts, instead of hugging it up and taking it for myself, I need to give it right back to the source. "Yours is the power. Yours is the glory," I say, trying not to hold on to it. If I ever make the mistake of stepping away from a stage without doing this, I will find myself wandering lost outside myself for days, like I'm being punished for being a glory thief. So these days right after I sing, I don't greet any fans and I don't talk to the press; I have to go to a quiet place where I can finish handing over the glory in private, and after I do that, I really, really need to eat.

My manager made room service bring up my supper – rice and peas, salad, and a big grilled snapper – and waited until I finished it off, fish head and all, before bringing this little girl, who he introduced to me as a journalist from London who wanted to interview me for a music magazine. I never did like doing interviews. To me, these press people usually have some axe or the other to grind; sometimes it's as if they write the whole story before, so you wonder why they even bother to come and talk to you. But I don't know why, when I look at this little English girl, my spirit just take her.

Thank you for what you said out there, that was very nice of you. Yes, yes, it really feels good to be on stage again after such a long time. If you listen to the words of "Dead and Wake," the song I opened the show with, if you listen to the lyrics, you'll understand how I feel, but what I'm really pleased about is that a whole new generation of young people like you are now appreciating my music. I have to give thanks to my manager over there for that.

That is true. My sound has changed and I'm not sure how you would classify it.

Some American musicians emailed me the other day to say they consider what I'm doing now to be a new kind of music.

"Mother of Mercy?" Yes, that song is my story. You were adopted? I ask because a lot of people who were adopted really like that song; but you know what, since over the years so many journalists put out their own version of what happened, let me tell it to you exactly how Miss Joyce, whom I call my grandmother, tell it to me. As she would say, "So me buy it, so me sell it." She said she was standing at a bus stop downtown one evening and a girl who looked like she could be about sixteen or so came up. She was carrying a baby, me, and Miss Joyce said the way she was holding me careless, with just one hand under my bottom and not using her other hand to support my back and my head, made you know that this was a case of a child having a child. Miss Joyce said she was so sorry for me that she started to make much of me:

"What a sweet baby, hello, little one, hello, precious, you cooing already? and you so small, coo again, make the old lady hear you."

And the young girl said:

"You can just hold her for me, lady? I twist mi ankle and mi shoe strap burst, and I just going over to the shoemaker to make him sew it up for me. I soon come back."

And Miss Joyce said, she said:

"Of course, darling. Just give her here to me, you have a clean napkin or a towel? Spread it cross my bosom, I don't want my dirty clothes to bump-up her skin."

And as far as I know that was the last anybody ever see of my mother after she spread that bird's-eye diaper across Miss Joyce's chest at the bus stop and limp off with her shoes strap slapping her ankle.

Miss Joyce? No, she never had any children herself, she was over forty when my mother pawn me off on her at the bus stop. She worked as a live-in domestic helper for a doctor and his wife. They had two sons, but they were away at boarding school in England. Everybody at the bus stop was telling her that she shouldn't take me.

"How a big woman like you going to manage a little baby? You have to make the government take her."

Well, that was what people was saying; but what Miss Joyce tell me that she was saying was:

"Imagine look how long I live on this earth and the Lord never see it fit to open my womb with a child, and just like that woman in the Bible I get a baby when I past child-bearing age and I never even have to go to lying-in and do hard labour."

"Mother of Mercy" is my thanks to Miss Joyce for not passing me on like a parcel after my mother give me away:

> It wasn't wrapped in pretty paper
> no shiny ribbons no sweet-words card,
> but you accepted the gift of me anyway
> took my presence right into to your heart,
> my mother, mother of mercy.

According to Miss Joyce, she always knew that I was going to be a singer because from the first evening she carried me home and put me down in the bed beside her, I just lay down right there in the dark with my two eyes wide open, looking around the little room, making my own sounds every time a song come over the radio.

No, nobody knows when I was really born, and at this stage of my life I like to think that is a secret that God will reveal to me personally one day. Miss Joyce just decided to call the day my mother gave me away my birthday, and every year she would send to the radio station and request birthday greetings for me.

Childhood memories? Well, one thing I'll always remember is that from I know myself, the first thing Miss Joyce would do every morning is to turn on her radio that was on a three-legged table behind the bed, and tune in to the early morning service. As a child I used to feel so safe when the two of us were lying down in her old-time iron bed under a little green blanket, with her hugging me up tight against her stomach keeping me warm.

Honest to God, Miss Joyce couldn't make the people she worked with know that she had a baby in the room with her, and so she hide me away like Pharaoh's daughter hide Moses. I stayed inside that little room most of the time until I was a big child who could walk and talk.

The first time the people who she worked with knew about me was when I was nearly three, and I disobeyed her and stepped outside into the yard to pick up a mango, and one of the doctor's sons who was home from school came round the back looking for the gardener and saw me. Yes, the gardener knew about me, but Miss Joyce was very kind to him and so he never said anything, as a matter of fact he was the nearest thing to a father I had when I was growing up. He was the one who nailed up two flat pieces of board across the doorway to keep me inside the room when I started to creep. His name was Wilfred and he used to keep pigeons and barbary doves in a big mesh wire cage. One of the first things I remember is me standing at the doorway of Miss Joyce's room looking out over the two pieces of board into the yard, which had a lot of mango and lime and breadfruit trees – it was "well fruited," as we Jamaicans would say. I remember looking out at the trees and hearing Wilfred's barbary doves calling and me trying to answer them.

How come they didn't know about me? You may not understand this, but I'm not even sure that those people even knew Miss Joyce's last name! To them she was just Joyce, or Cookie. I mean, they used to call Wilfred, who must have been over fifty, "the yard boy." I don't think they knew his last name either, and they never came around to "the maid's quarters," which was way off to itself round the back of this really big house.

No, she said I was a really quiet baby, that it's like I knew from the first that I had to really make myself small and not give any trouble. Miss Joyce would only bring me outside if the doctor and his wife were not there, and as soon as she heard the car drive up and the doctor start blowing the car horn for Wilfred to come and open the gate, she would run and put me back inside the room.

If she was really busy in the kitchen, she said she would have to leave me alone in the room for the whole day with just a feeding bottle of cornmeal porridge with a big hole cut out in the nipple for me to drink the porridge through, in the bed with me. She fenced in the bed with two old chairs so that I wouldn't roll off on to the floor and she turned on the radio to keep my company.

Later on when I could walk. I used to stand and put my face up to the round wire mesh panel at the front of the radio so that I could really get close to the songs and to the announcers' voices.

After the doctor's son saw me picking up the mango, Miss Joyce carried me into the big house and introduced me as her little niece from the country who was spending time with her.

Maybe because by this time — according to what Miss Joyce told me when I was big — the doctor and his wife were sleeping in different bedrooms because they were well on their way to a divorce, they never said anything about me staying with her.

Also I was so happy to come out of that little room that from the day I set foot in that big fabulous house — the kitchen was three times the size of Miss Joyce's room and the fridge was way bigger than the press that Miss Joyce hang up her clothes in, which was the biggest thing in that maid's room — I started to work hard to make everybody like me.

If anybody drop anything I would run and pick it up and hand it to them, and if I noticed the doctor or his wife or anybody looking at me, I'd start to sing, usually some song that I heard on the radio. After a time I was a real little mascot, me. Maybe I just know from early that I was going to have to sing for my supper. One day I heard the doctor's wife say, "We should take her down to the circus, she is a real little monkey." Everybody laughed when she said that.

Because Miss Joyce had arthritis, she made me help her in the kitchen, I learned to clean seasoning and shell peas and do little things for her almost from the first day she brought me into the kitchen. What I'll never forget is how when I started washing my own clothes, she used to put me to sit down on a little bench and she used to say, "Patti, take it as I tell you, if you sing when you washing you surprise to see how quick you finish."

How can I describe Miss Joyce to you now.

Well some people might say she was not a good-looking lady. Although her complexion was dark and smooth like molasses, her face was . . . it was kinda long. Her nose, her mouth, even her gums long, only her teeth short; and she had what she herself used to call a "K foot," which is what Jamaicans call knock knees. But to me, she just looked like Miss Jamaica. She had this loving little sideway look that she used to give me sometimes, especially when I had to start bathing her because of the arthritis. She would just look at me with so much love, her eyes brim full of water when she, a big woman, had to stand up there stark naked with her two arms up in the air like she was surrendering, to make me, a little girl, soap up her skin. I used to climb up on to the same little bench that I sit down on to wash, and when I hold up the goblet high and pour out the water to rinse her off, she shut her eyes tight and the two of us would sing:

> It's coming down down down it's coming down
> and the glory of the lord is coming down

The little maid's room always smelled of liniment and bay rum, but anytime I asked Miss Joyce if we could open a window to let in some cool breeze, she would say, "Child, you want me catch cold and dead?" If you come to my house in Portland, which to me is the most beautiful parish in Jamaica, you will see that I don't have one window closed. I'm sure that is because of all the years I spend in that little room.

I wrote my first real song when I was about sixteen, and I honestly wish I could tell you that it was because I was inspired by the smell of flowers or that the sight of the sun going down over the Caribbean sea moved me so much that the words just overflowed onto a page in my school exercise book.

So what it was you asked me again? Oh, what inspired me to write my first song? Okay. When I went to school I always loved poetry. The doctor that Miss Joyce worked for was a decent man, and one day when I was about four or so, he came into the kitchen and saw me sitting down on my little bench with a basin in my lap, shelling green gungoo peas. I used to like to mash the soft little green worms that curl up inside the pods, and every time I squash one of them I would sing this little song that I made up:

> *goodbye, little worm,*
> *goodbye, little worm,*
> *go home to your mum,*
> *go home to your mum.*

The doctor thought this was very funny and he said to Miss Joyce, "Joyce, your niece is a bright little girl, and since it looks as she is never going back to the country, you better send her to school so she can make something of herself." I went to infant school, then to primary school when I was seven; I passed my common entrance and I got a free place to high school when I was eleven.

The people in Miss Joyce's church used to help to buy my books and uniforms, and the doctor used to give me lunch money and busfare and every Christmas he would buy books of poems and stories and give them to me. All through school I was always in the choir or in some choral speaking group.

I memorized lots of poems, and I know the words to hymns. Maybe that is why writing songs come so easily to me.

I wrote my first song, "Black but Comely" to throw back words on people.

"Tell them you black but you comely, that is what the Queen of Sheba tell Solomon." Miss Joyce said I was to tell that to some children at school. You know what they were calling me? Little Orphan Blacky.

> *I am black but comely — cool black and smooth.*
> *My eyes are big — large, to hold the stars in my eyeballs.*
> *My hair is knotty — thick, I don't have to wear a wig.*
> *My lips are thick — wide and big, all the better to sing with.*
> *My nose is flat — but not flat like your mind is.*

First real song I ever wrote. Write it when I was about sixteen to throw back words on all the people, some teachers at school, people in the church, people who were just determined that I was not to ever fly past my nest and forget that I come from nowhere, that my own mother never even want me, that she give away to a stranger woman at a bus stop who had to hide me from the world for years.

Chuh, if all she can sing, me must can sing too. One girl at my school actually said that.

Can you imagine that? Listen, from the time I started to sing along with the songs on the radio, from the first time Miss Joyce started taking me with her to church and I join in with the choir until one night the choir started to follow me, I just know that that is what I came into this world to do.

Yes, I sing big. I like big singing. You know how some people sing a song like they're mean with it, swallow part of it and keep it for themself and then lend you the rest? Not me. When I sing, I give everything.

Yes, my first big break came when I won the Opportunity Knocks talent competition. Yes, Miss Joyce encouraged me to enter. Of course I was nervous! It was the first big audience I ever performed before, but I knew in my heart, nobody had to tell me, that if I looked into that big Kingston crowd I was going to turn to stone up there on that stage, so all the time I was up on there I hold on to a handkerchief with my bus fare back to Stony Hill knot up in one corner. It was a white lace handkerchief that Miss Joyce sprinkled with some of her Evening in Paris perfume, and I wrap it round my left hand and pull at one of the corners with my right hand, and I picture myself in the little room in the maid's quarters, me and my grandmother Miss Joyce with the radio turn up high till the knob buck and can't go any farther, and I imagine that I was making my voice come out through the radio . . .

First prize. $2,000 and a recording contract.

I win for Miss Joyce, who used put her hand on top of my head and say: "One day, one day, your voice going to come over the radio."

Although I was always grateful to Miss Joyce for everything she ever did for me, I never had the heart to tell her that even from I was small I couldn't take the sound of that singing rage Miss Patti Page. You couldn't turn on the radio without hearing that singing rage Miss Patti Page. I just didn't understand how a doggy could be for sale in a window, I just could not picture it. I never liked Patti Page water-crackers voice because I always liked big singing. I feel that is how people should sing, as if they really mean it.

By the time we had two radio stations that eventually started to play Jamaican music, you would only hear one or two women singers and the best of them was Hortense Ellis.

Yes, I did meet her. When I just started out I actually had the honour of singing with Hortense on a show called *Ladies Night*. Let me tell you, when Hortense stepped out onto the stage, you see, in a maroon and royal blue African gown with a head tie to match! mercy! that woman school every other female singer on that show that night. She was a fine-looking woman, she was black and, not but, black *and* comely.

I say the woman carried herself like a queen. I was watching her backstage and I observed how she just stood up quiet before she went on stage. It was as if she was in a trance. She didn't make a sound, she didn't talk to anybody until she step onto that stage and then! as Miss Joyce would say, "What a mashallaw!" She never missed a beat, she never once went off-key, as you young people today would say, She killed! until all the other performers – like me who were scheduled to come on later in the show – started to fret!

"Miss Ellis, I'm very honoured to meet you. I'm one of your biggest fans." Hortense throw back her head and laugh when I said that.

"My fan? What you talking bout, little girl, you are the big star now."

Imagine, Hortense Ellis said that to me.

Yes, I agree, she never did get her due because this music business is a boys' club.

Look how long Hortense was singing, and she passed on with hardly anything to show for it. And in those early days it was even worse than now. From producer who you have to pay with everything you have before you can go into the studio; disc jockey who want to play with you before your record can get airplay, to the public who believe that everything you do is their business. If you ever hear some of the facety things that some complete strangers feel free to come up and say to you because they buy one of you records one time!

Here is another thing, most men don't like their women to be "stars." They love you for it, but they hate you because of it. Ask almost any woman singer in this business and they will tell you the same story. But me, I love the same way I sing, totally and completely and I wish I could say, "*Non, je ne regrette rien*" but that would not be true. Yes, I love Edith Piaf. They used to play "Non, Je ne Regrette Rien" on the radio when I was growing up and everytime Dwight Whylie played it, he would explain the meaning of the words.

Much as I love that song, I cannot sing it, for there are still quite a few things in my life that I still regret, but you know, what I have in me is like a waterfall. A waterfall that is just pouring out itself from a high place, and although over the years it was getting beat up on the rocks, I always hoped that one day if I was lucky, I would find everything I poured out, collected up nice and peaceful in a clean pretty pool of water, and that anybody who was weary could come and just come refresh themself right there. But this recording business! Jesus, Mary, and Joseph, what a hard business!

I was wondering when you were going to mention him. Yes, he was my first producer and he is the father of my children. I signed up with him after I won the contest. At first it was star treatment all the way. Man moved me to Kingston, tell me to stop taking bus, send car and driver for me to go everywhere, send me to Miami to buy hundreds of dollars of clothes to wear on stage, me who hardly wear a new dress till I was big enough to make one for myself in sewing class at school. It was a purple dress, with a V-neck, and everybody said how the colour suited me, tall for my age, me, slim-body me, because believe me I grow on a diet of "what-left" from the doctor's kitchen, or as you would say "leftovers." I started to dress like a model and every journalist came and interviewed me for the newspaper but nobody was really interested in the fact that I write my own songs.

My First Hit?

I will never forget how I felt. To this day, "I feel like jumping," as Marcia Griffiths would say, whenever I remember Don Topping saying on the radio: "And now, a hot newie from the winner of the Opportunity Knocks talent contest; 'Big Love Girl' . . . this one is headed straight for the top sugar boo."

What do I think of Marcia? I think she is brilliant. She and Judy Mowatt are world-class singers, world class, the best that ever come out of Jamaica.

But as I was saying, I remember the first time I heard my record on the air. I jump up and down and scream out,

"Miss Joyce, you hear me over the radio?" And then I was surprised to hear myself saying, "My mother, who throw me away, you hear me over the radio? Me, me, Little Orphan Blacky, me black and me comely me, my song playing on the radio!"

Everybody in Jamaica was singing my songs and I was on every stage show. By Christmas of that year I was doing gigs in New York, and Toronto, Miami, Nassau. I did quite a few shows in London and later on I did a European tour.

Two children, a boy and a girl. I didn't really plan to have any at first because everything was going great for me in the first two years after the talent show, but I was living with my producer, who was old enough to be my father, in this big house in Vineyard Town. All kinds of things went on in that house, things I just learned to turn a blind eye to. I know this sounds bad, but I was never really in love with him, I just appreciated how he just took charge of everything. I liked that I never had to worry about any of the details. All I had to do was get ready and go into the studio or go onstage. I guess because of my circumstances you could say he was a father figure, I don't know. I just really liked the idea of somebody taking care of business for me so that I can just concentrate fully on my music.

I had one child for him and then another one after that. And right after I had the second one, all the good treatment I used to get from him just dry up. Vanish. It's only later I found out that while I was pregnant with my daughter he was becoming heavily involved with his new protégée, Lady X. After a while I used to wonder if this man got a calling to come and mad me because everytime something don't work out for him, like a foreign contract fall through, or one of his singers get caught up in some bandooloo business or the other, I am the one who would feel it.

"If it wasn't for me, you would still be living up there in the bush where only bull frog and toad can hear you when you sing."

Always, him always reminding me how I come from nothing, how if it wasn't for him I would still be nothing. You know when I was with him I used to dream that a man who looked like Jesus would come to me and tell me how I was nothing, and that not even he, Jesus, could want me. I used to believe that if Jesus who loved even lepers didn't want me, well then . . . but I guess I've learned that there is such a thing as an evil spirit. A spirit who will try to deceive you even in dreams. I get a lot of wisdom and inspiration through dreams, and I guess there is only one gate that these things come through, so in the same way the spirit of inspiration can visit me, deceiving spirits can come too.

One night after an award show when my record didn't win anything, my producer, who is the father of my children, drove off from the theatre and left me and my son standing in the carpark. It was a good thing my daughter, who a baby then, was with one of my friends. Drive off! Just because my record didn't win some blasted award. That night when I stood up outside in that carpark I never exactly cursed God, but I had to ask him some hard questions, "Is what I do so?" My own mother give me away and now I give this man so much, all something that I never know I have, I find them and give to him and this is what I get for it.

No, the copyright case has still not been resolved.

The man still has control over at least twenty of my songs because I was stupid enough to make him take credit as co-writer with me. Co-write what? You have to understand that he was the big, experienced producer, so when he put the suggestion to me that since nobody really knew me as a song-writer, it would be better if we put down the two of us as co-writers, even though that man never wrote one word in any of those songs, I just went along with it. If it wasn't for my son, maybe I might have just ended up as another mad woman wandering the streets of Kingston that night, but when I started to listen to what I call my orphan voice, telling me that I was nothing and that I was never going to be anything but nothing, my boy said, "Mamma, lift me up," and just as I picked him up, the manager of the theatre came out and saw us out there in the carpark and gave us a lift home.

I recorded with three different labels after I left the father of my children and honestly, I would have to say that at least half of the people I deal with in this business robbed me or carried me down at one time or the other. Except for the young dread over there, who is my manager and who must be one of the few honest, upright people in this business, almost everyone I ever deal with in this recording business turn out to be another one who come to mad me. It's a wonder I never really and truly mad because, believe me, I come close. Close close. The last man I was along with before everything in my life changed was a man who I met after I spent three years without anybody.

I was wringing down wet after I performed for one and a half hours straight. You know how some singers come on, sing two or three songs, then force everybody to sing along with them; in other words, you pay to see them, but you must do the work? I never force an audience to sing with me. If you want to sing, I say, Feel free, but as far as I am concerned, if you leave your house and pay to come and hear me, I am the one who is supposed to be doing the singing. I made up my mind from the time I started in this business that I would never shortchange my audience. Three encores I got that night; and the blue sequin gown that I was wearing weighed ninety-nine pounds on me because it was soaked right through with sweat. When I stepped backstage this fine-looking man just appeared out of the darkness with a white towel.

"Please, give me the honour of wiping your beautiful face, my princess."

What could I do? I just stand there and let him gently wipe my face like a mother.

After that, everywhere I turn, this man, he's an entertainer too, was there. And if I was on before him, him was always there to wipe my face when I come off stage, to give me a glass of ice water, to ask me how I was getting home, to offer to take me home.

Well, as it happens this man didn't believe in birth control, and I really should have known better. I got pregnant, and this same person who was so tenderly stepping out of the backstage darkness to wipe my face, this man who claimed to be a righteous man who put his hand on the Bible and swear that all he wanted to do was to honour me, the same man him looked into my face and asked me if I sure it was his.

Women write to me all the time asking me what my song "Little Bird" is really about. I tell them to take it any way they want, but just let me say that I decided not to have a third child. I just could not see any other way; it was either that or have it and give it away like my mother give me away, and I just couldn't do that.

> *My little bird you take flight*
> *go on be one now with the night.*
> *When I fly past this pain,*
> *we'll be birds of one feather again.*

Miss Joyce always said that God has our tears in a bottle; my bottle must be a demijohn. You know what that same man who appeared out of the darkness with the towel and wiped my face said to me one time?

"You make me feel guilty because I can't live up to you. I feel really bad when I do you the smallest little thing."

But I said, "I am a human being and I know I have my bad ways too." I don't expect that two people trying to pull together not going to have problems.

Hear him: "Yes, but when I hear you sing I just can't live up to you. You see your talent? It come in like baby mole, I don't want to damage it. It's better I leave it alone." And so said, so done. He left me quite alone.

A baby's mole? That is that soft, tender place at the top of a baby's head.

After that happened though, I learned to watch what people do and not what they look like or what they say. I can honestly tell you now that I don't care about the colour of anybody's skin, or what church they go to, or who they sleep with. All I care about is how sincere a person is, and if they treat me just like they would like somebody to treat them.

No, I was never into drugs. But I used to drink hard and I smoked a pack and a half of cigarettes a day. Those blues singers who smoked, you can hear it in their voices, Billy Holiday, Carmen McCrae, the two of them were smokers. I love Carmen's voice, it just sounds haunting, like she was coming through a valley all by herself. I caught her at Ronnie Scott's in London one night. Her parents were Jamaican, you know.

Yes, I lived in London for a while. I left my children with a friend for one year and that is another story right there. But I was making good money, doing gigs all over Europe. Europeans love my music, they say I remind them of Nina Simone, but what I mostly remember from those days was that I was keeping some bad company, hanging out with some hard-living people in this business; people who live life backways, sleep all day and come alive only at night. I started to look old before my time, and I got bad pneumonia so I came back to Jamaica.

Yes, Miss Joyce was still alive then, she had stopped working and as the doctor's wife – by this time he was dead – immigrated to Miami during the 1970s, without giving her even one dollar for severance pay, she moved back to Portland where she had a piece of family land and I sent money for her to build a house – that is the same place where I live now – and I paid a lady to look after her. But I'm ashamed to say that a lot of times I was so involved in my own drama that sometimes months passed before I would go and look for her. I will always feel bad about the fact that I personally never really took better care of her.

Why did I change my name?

As I told you, Miss Joyce named me after her favourite singer, Patti Page, but in Jamaica a patty, as I'm sure you know, is something like what you call a cornish pasty. So I changed my name to Shekinah. I like that it means tranquillity.

Bob Marley? Well, I personally owe Bob Marley a big debt. No, I didn't work with him or anything, but seriously, Bob Marley helped save my life.

How? Well, one Saturday evening I was at home watching TV with my children and a program about Bob Marley came on. It was a rerun, and Neville Willoughby, one of Miss Joyce's favourite announcers, was interviewing Bob, who was explaining why he left the music business and took up farming.

I nearly dropped off the couch! Bob Marley? Bob Marley of all people left the music business? I never knew that had happened! But apparently at that time, everything was going against him. The big producers carrying him down, the radio station refusing to play his records – Bob hardly had a number-one hit in Jamaica, just imagine that! The newspapers were not taking him seriously because in those days people in Jamaica had no respect whatsoever for anything named Rasta. Police used to beat them and cut off their hair. You know, if you had come to Jamaica, say, thirty years ago with your hair locks up like that, it would have been a big disgrace.

If children had locks they wouldn't admit them into school, I'm dead serious.

You, me, my manager, and everybody else who wear locks freely now, owe those early Rastas a big debt.

But as I was telling you, it was as if all the forces of darkness were just lined up against Bob, and rather than stay there and allow them to destroy him, he just turned his back on everything and everybody and went back to country. As long as I live, I will never forget the sight of Bob Marley, who is now one of the biggest stars who ever pass through this universe, leading a donkey through a banana walk.

As if that was not enough of a sign, I went to bed that night and dreamed that I saw a woman at the foot of a hill, her head was pointing down and her two legs were pointing up the hill. When I looked around her head was resting in a pile of garbage . . . a whole heap of rotten stinking rubbish. Even in the dream I could smell it . . . it was like the garbage of everybody in the world that she was lying down in, it was so rotten and so plenty. Then around her was a ring of dogs with ribs that look like scrubbing board and the dogs just hankering round her and the garbage, to me, it looked like they were waiting for her death. And like a flash reach me . . . like I see myself . . . as if it was really me lying down there, for to tell the truth, my life was like a pile of stinking garbage. I owe money, a mad woman was threatening to kill me – she claimed that I took away her man – because all her idiot boyfriend was doing night and day was singing my songs and looking at a picture of me that he cut out from the newspaper. Every time I made a record they played it two times on the radio, then stop because I didn't have money for payola. The last two times I performed the promoter disappeared without paying me one cent.

My name was at the top of the agenda at every meeting in J.P.'s Hairdressing Parlour, where barracudas gather to wash their hair and wash their mouth on other women. She done with, "She mash up, you see!" As for the friends: according to Miss Joyce, when you dream about a dog, that means a friend. Well, my friends were really just frenemy. As Peter Tosh would say, "mawgre dogs" who were jealous of my talent. There was even one who used to say to me that true friends should be "on the same level" at all times. So if she was broke and had to be living on the street because she wasted every chance that life sent her way – as a friend, I should make sure that I was broke and homeless too. Don't that is madness? And that was one of my closest friends. Another one who was trying to pass off herself as a singer actually had the nerve to tell me one day that I should stop singing, that I sing enough already, and that she wanted to sing now! I realized after a while that all of them were just waiting for me to crash and burn, but I learned one thing, take it as I tell you, it's better to be alone than to be in bad company.

Many of my songs do come to me in dreams, that is true.

I have a song about that dream with the mawgre dogs. It's on my new album, it's called "Make a Way." I guess this was a kind of dream inside a dream, but at some point when I was having that dream about me lying down in the rubbish, I'd remembered something Miss Joyce used to say . . . when life looked like it out to tumble down on her she would say loud, loud "Lord, make a way." In the dream I said, "Lord, make a way," and in the dream it was like a way opened in the garbage, and I found strength and I kicked away some of it myself and I got a stone and I fling it after the dogs and scatter them. And I find myself standing up and when I look to my right, there was this big clean pool of water. It looked like nobody ever bathed in there. It looked blue as if, if God has a ring, that is the colour of the stone in the ring. And I took off all my clothes and I bathe and I bathe and I bathe. I wash out my clothes and I spread them on the grass to dry and I bathe until night come down, and the moon come out with her big round face.

And the moon carried a lot of stars with her and she dressed up the sky with them and so I got all the light that I needed to walk up the hill.

When I wake, I was crying. I was crying so much I was really in a pool.

Let me ask you a question now. You know how to heed your signs? Your hints? as some people call them. Well, dear, take it as I tell you, you would be wise to start paying attention to things like that. In my case I couldn't want two clearer signs. If Bob Marley, Bob Marley of all people, could walk away and leave this music business, if I could get a dream like that, that I was lying down in garbage, what plainer sign could I want?

The morning after I had that dream, I got up and I went down to Portland. I spent the most part of one whole day sitting down on Miss Joyce's tomb, telling her how sorry I was that I made vanity just take over my life. I told her how sorry I was that I wasn't even there when she passed, because when I got the message that she was sick, I was singing in some fly-by-night nightclub in Miami and because I believed that gig would lead to a big recording contract (which never did materialize), when I got the message that she had a stroke, I didn't get on a plane right away and come right back to see her before she closed her eyes.

I got down on my knees beside her tomb and begged her pardon. I asked her to help me from wherever she was because I wanted my life to change. Even if my voice never came over the radio again. Even if I never stepped on to a stage again in life. Even if nobody ever call me "star" or beg me for an autograph, or tell me how much my music mean to them, I didn't care. And even if all these years I was really hoping that my birth mother would hear me singing and come back and throw herself down before me and beg me pardon for giving me away at a bus stop. And that my father – whoever, and wherever he was – would come with her too, and kiss the ground before me and beg me pardon, that was never, ever going to happen. Even if I was feeling so great that all the people who used to call me Little Orphan Blacky were now claiming that me and them were the very best of friends because they used to go to school with me, so what? All I want is a decent life. I want my children to respect me, I want to stop leaving them here and there for people to ill treat them while I go and chase some big chance that was always slipping away from me.

Help me, help me, help me with the mawgre dog and the rubbish I am in, help me, help me, help me.

> *My sistren, remember*
> *that you and me,*
> *we are only channels*
> *and vessels*
> *through which the creator's*
> *glory passes.*

I swear that I heard Bob Marley's voice singing that. Right after I called out, "Help me, help me, help me." I never could figure out how Bob Marley's voice was coming to me from out of Miss Joyce's tomb, but I guess that's how spirit is, spirit just makes it own kind of sense. And then I heard Bob singing again:

> *Do like me, friend of mine*
> *and take back your pearls*
> *from before the swine,*
> *for a season, for a time.*

I stopped singing after I moved down to Portland. For years and years, not even when I washed clothes I didn't sing, I never even moan the words of a hymn like Miss Joyce used to moan them, until one day I opened my mouth and the new singing and the new way of being in the world that you hear and see in me now just started to pour out of me like a waterfall.

The following stories appeared in *Baby Mother and the King of Swords*, published by Longman U.K. in 1990: "Bella Makes Life," "By Love Possessed," "God's Help" (formerly "Follow Your Mind"), "House Colour" (formerly "I Don't Want to Go Home in the Dark"), "The Big Shot," "Pinky's Fall," "The Dolly Funeral," "Angelita and Golden Days," "Shilling," and "I Come Through."

The story "By Love Possessed" received The Pushcart Prize and also appeared in the 1995 collection *Ancestral House*, edited by Charles Rowell.

The following stories appeared in *Fool-Fool Rose Is Leaving Labour-In-Vain Savannah*, published by Ian Randle Publishers, Kingston, Jamaica, in 2005: "Jamaica Hope," "Henry," "Wedding in Roxbury," "Fool-Fool Rose Is Leaving Labour-In-Vain Savannah," "Talola's Husband," "Alice and the Dancing Angel," "For My Comrades Wearing Three-Piece Suits," "Dream Lover," "Miss Henny, Suliman Santer, and Me," and "Mi Amiga Gran."

Most of these stories have been substantially revised for this book.

"The Helpweight" and "Don't Sit on the Beauty Seat" appear here for the first time.

ACKNOWLEDGEMENTS

To Dawn Davis, who is a class act. Thank you for your gracious and continuing faith in my work.

To Ellen Seligman with sincerest gratitude for convincing me to revisit these stories.

To Ron Eckel with many thanks for all he does to get the word out.

To Shanna Milkey and Kendra Ward for all their help and patience.

To Kate and Ed West for their nurturing friendship and support.

To Dean Terrence McDonald, Nicolas Delbanco, Lincoln Faller, Sid Smith, Michael Schoenfeldt, Larry Goldstein, George Bornstein, Eileen Pollack, Linda Gregerson, Patsy Yaeger, Michael Awkward, Theresa Tinkle, Evans Young, Ralph Williams, John Whittier-Ferguson, and all my colleagues at the University of Michigan. Thanks for your help and support over the years.

To my siblings: Barbara, Howard, Betty, Vaughn, Kingsley and Karl, Keith and Nigel. Storytellers all.

ABOUT THE AUTHOR

Lorna Goodison is an internationally renowned poet and the author of the highly acclaimed memoir *From Harvey River*, a book hailed as "captivating" in the *New York Times* and named a *Washington Post Book World* Best Book of the Year. She is the recipient of the Musgrave Gold Medal and the Commonwealth Writers Prize, among other accolades. Her work has been widely translated and anthologized in major collections of contemporary poetry. Born in Jamaica, she now teaches at the University of Michigan.

WITHDRAWN
No longer the property of the
Boston Public Library.
Sale of this material benefits the Library